Table of Contents

THE AMPHIBIAN MAN

Alexander Belyaev

Translation and cover art by Maria K. with images provided by 123RF
Editing by Pubright Manuscript Services

*****

PUBLISHED BY:

TSK Group LLC

THE AMPHIBIAN MAN

Copyright © 2013 by TSK Group LLC

Kindle Edition License Notes

PART ONE

"THE SEA DEVIL"

It was a stuffy January night of Argentinian summer. Stars shone brightly in the black sky. Medusa stood anchored and still. Neither the splashing of waves nor creaking of the rigging broke the silence of the night. The ocean seemed to be sound asleep.

The half-naked pearl divers were sprawled on the deck of the schooner. Tired from the day of work and from the heat, they rolled over, gasped and cried out in their heavy sleep. Their arms and legs twitched nervously. Perhaps they were dreaming about their sworn enemies – the sharks. During these hot windless days people got so tired that they couldn't eve raise the boats after the day's dive. Although, this was unnecessary – nothing indicated a change in weather. And so the boats remained in the water overnight, tied to the anchor chain. The halyards were askew, the cables – poorly tightened, the jib was left to flutter lightly in the weak breeze. The entire deck between the forecastle and quarterdeck was covered in piles of pearl oysters, bits of coral, ropes for lowering the divers to the bottom of the sea, canvas sacks for the shells, and empty barrels. Next to the mizzen stood a large barrel with fresh water and an iron pitcher attached to it by a chain. The deck around the barrel was stained dark from the spilled water.

From time to time one of the divers rose, rocking in his half-sleep and stumbled to the water barrel stepping on the hands and feet of the others. Without opening his eyes, he drank a pitcher of water and collapsed as if he wasn't drinking water but pure alcohol. The divers were thirsty. It was dangerous to eat in the morning, before work – the pressure they were subject to underwater was too high for that. That is why they worked all day on an empty stomach, until it was too dark to dive. They could only eat before going to sleep, and all they had was cured meat.

Balthazar, the Indian, kept watch at night. He was the closest assistant to Captain Pedro Zurita, the owner of the schooner *Medusa*.

In his youth, Balthazar was a famous pearl diver – he could spend ninety or even a hundred seconds underwater, which was twice longer than normal.

1

"Why? Because in my day, they knew how to teach and they started teaching us since childhood," Balthazar told the young divers. "I was a ten-year old kid when my father sent me to apprentice with Jose. He had twelve of us. Here is how he taught us. He threw a white rock or a seashell into the water and ordered, 'Go get it!' Every time he threw it deeper and deeper. If you didn't get it he beat you with a rope or a whip and threw you back in the water like a pup. 'Try again!' That was how we learned to dive. Then he started teaching us to stay underwater longer. He was an old experienced diver. He dove to the bottom and tied a basket or a net to the anchor. And then we had to dive and untie it underwater. We weren't supposed to surface until we were done. If we did – we were once again treated to the whip.

"We were beaten ruthlessly. Not many of us could stand it. But I became the best diver in the district and earned good money."

When he grew old, Balthazar left the dangerous profession of a pearl diver. His left leg was torn by a shark's teeth, his side was scratched by an anchor chain. He had a small shop on Buenos Aires, where he sold pearls, coral, seashells, and various sea curiosities. But he grew bored ashore and frequently joined the pearl diving parties. The shop owners valued him. No one knew the La Plata Bay better than Balthazar, including its shorelines and places with the most pearl oysters. Other divers respected him. He knew how to stay in good graces with everyone – both the divers and the owners.

He taught the secrets of his craft to the young divers – how to hold their breath, how to defend against sharks, and, if he was in a good mood – how to hide a rare pearl from the master.

The shop owners knew and appreciated him for his unmistakable knack for rating pearls and the ability to sort the best ones out for the captain.

Thus, they gladly took him along as an assistant and an advisor.

Balthazar sat on an empty barrel and slowly smoked a fat cigar. The light from the lantern attached to the mast fell onto his face. It was elongated, but without the high cheekbones, with a straight nose and large beautiful eyes – a typical Arauca face. Balthazar's eyelids drooped heavily, then lifted slowly. He dozed off. But while his eyes were asleep, his ears were awake. They were alert and warned about danger even when he was sound asleep. But presently, Balthazar heard only the sighs and mumbling of the sleeping men. The smell of the rotting pearl oysters wafted from the shore – they were left to rot to make it easier to pick out the pearls, because the shells of the living oysters were difficult to open. This smell would have seemed revolting to a regular person, but Balthazar inhaled it with some pleasure. The smell reminded him, the vagrant and the pearl hunter, of the joys of free life and the exciting dangers of the sea.

After the pearls were picked out, the largest shells would be transported to *Medusa*.

Zurita was pragmatic – he sold the shells to a factory, where they were made into buttons and cufflinks.

Balthazar was asleep. His cigar fell from his relaxed fingers, and his head tipped down onto his chest.

Suddenly, his consciousness was touched by a sound coming somewhere from the ocean. The sound came closer. Balthazar opened his eyes. Someone seemed to have blown into a trumpet and then a young human voice shouted, "Ah!" and again, an octave higher, "A-a-a-ah!"

The trumpet sound was nothing like the abrupt steamer siren, and the merry voice didn't sound like a drowning person screaming for help. This was something new, something unknown. Balthazar rose; the air seemed to have grown cooler. He walked over to the railing and peered at the smooth surface of the ocean. It was deserted. And quiet. Balthazar nudged another Indian sprawled on the deck with his foot, and when the latter rose, he said quietly, "Someone is shouting. It must be *him*."

"I can't hear anything," the Huron man replied, standing on his knees and listening. The silence was once again broken by the trumpet sound and another shout, "A-a-h!"

The Huron heard it and pitched forward as if someone struck him with a whip.

"Yes, it must be him," the Huron said, his teeth chattering in terror. Other divers woke up too. They crawled to the area lit by the lantern, as if looking for protection from the darkness in the weak circle of yellowish light. Everyone sat huddling together and listening. The trumpet sound and the voice repeated in the distance, and then everything was silent.

"It's *him*…"

"The Sea Devil," the divers whispered.

"We can't stay here any longer!"

"It's worse than any shark!"

3

"Get the master here!"

They heard the padding of bare feet. Yawning and scratching his hairy chest, the owner, Pedro Zurita, appeared on deck. He was shirtless and wore a pair of canvas pants with a revolver holster on his wide leather belt. Zurita walked up to the divers. The lantern revealed his sleepy face, bronze-colored from the tan, thick curly hair falling on his forehead, black eyebrows, abundant bristling mustache and a small graying goatee.

"What is the matter?"

His calm, slightly coarse voice and confident movements calmed the Indians.

They all started talking at once. Balthazar raised his hand to make them stop and said, "We heard his voice... the Sea Devil."

"You imagined it!" Pedro replied sleepily, his head drooping.

"No, we didn't. We all heard a shout and a trumpet sound!" the divers shouted.

With the same hand gesture, Balthazar once again ordered them to be quiet and continued, "I heard it myself. Only the Devil makes that sound. Nobody else in the sea shouts and trumpets like that. We must leave here."

"Fairy tales," Pedro Zurita replied just as listlessly.

He really did not want to load the stinky half-rotten shells onto the boat and move.

But there was no reasoning with the Indians. They were agitated, they were gesticulating and shouting, threatening to go ashore the next morning and walk to Buenos Aires, if Zurita refused to move.

"Damn this Sea Devil and you with him! Fine. We shall sail at dawn." Still grumbling, the captain went back to his quarters.

He was no longer sleepy. He lit an oil lamp, found a cigar and started pacing around his small room. He thought about the mysterious creature that appeared recently in the local waters, frightening fishermen and other locals.

No one had seen this monster, but it made its presence known several times. Fables were told about it. Sailors told the stories in whispers, glancing around furtively, as if afraid that the monster might be eavesdropping.

The creature caused harm to some and provided unexpected help to others. "It's a sea god," old Indians said. "He comes from the ocean once every thousand years to restore justice on earth."

Catholic priests assured the superstitious Spaniards that it was the "sea devil." He appeared because people started forgetting the good old Catholic church.

All these rumors passed by word of mouth finally reached Buenos Aires. For several weeks the Sea Devil became the favorite topic of the reporters and satirists working for the local tabloids. When shops and fishing boats sank under strange circumstances, or fishing nets were cut, or the day's catch vanished, the Sea Devil was blamed. But others said that the Devil sometimes threw large fish into the fishermen's boats and once even rescued a drowning man.

At least one man assured that when he went underwater, someone caught him behind his back and swam to the shore, supporting him the entire way. The stranger vanished in the surf the moment the rescued man stepped on the shore.

The strangest thing was that no one managed to see the Devil himself. No one could describe what this mysterious creature looked like. There were "witnesses", of course – they said that the Devil had horns, a goat's beard, a lion's paws and the tail of a fish. Or else they portrayed him as a giant horned toad with human legs.

The government officials of Buenos Aires paid no attention to these stories and news articles, considering them to be nothing but a hoax.

But the anxiety continued to grow, primarily among the fishermen. Many of them didn't dare go out into the sea. The catch being brought in dropped and people started feeling a fish deficit. Then the local government decided to investigate this situation. Several steam launches and motor boats belonging to the local coast guard were dispatched along the coastline with the orders to "detain the unknown person causing confusion and panic among the local population." The police searched the La Plata Bay and shores for two weeks, arrested several Indians for spreading false rumors and causing trouble, but the Devil himself escaped.

The chief of police published an official statement that there was no Devil, and it was nothing but fairy tales spread by ignorant people, who had already been detained and would be punished accordingly. He tried to convince the fishermen to ignore the rumors and get back to fishing.

This helped for a time. However, the Devil's pranks weren't over.

One night, the fishermen who were fairly far away from the shore were awakened by the bleating of a baby goat, which miraculously appeared aboard their longboat. Other fishermen found their nets cut up.

Thrilled by the Devil's new appearance, the reporters waited for an explanation from the scientists.

The scientists didn't keep them waiting long.

They believed that there could not be an unknown sea monster living in the ocean and carrying out actions only a human being was capable of. "It would have been different," the scientists wrote, "if such a creature appeared in the poorly explored areas of the ocean." Still, the scientists refused to admit that this creature could act intelligently. Along with the chief of police and the coast guard, they believed that these were pranks carried out by some mischief maker.

But not everyone thought that.

Another group of scientists cited the famous Swiss naturalist Conrad Gessner who lived in the 16th century and wrote the famous *History of Animals* that influenced zoologist greatly for a long time. Gessner described the sea maiden, the sea devil, the sea monk, and the sea bishop.

"After all, much of what was written by the ancient and medieval scientist has been proven to be true, despite the fact that modern science refused to recognize these old teachings. God's creativity is limitless, and it would behoove us, scientists, to be humble and careful in our conclusions more than anyone else," some of the older scientists wrote.

In truth, it was difficult to describe these humble and cautious people as scientists. They believed in miracles more than in science, and their lectures were akin to sermons. When all was said and done, in order to resolve this argument, a scientific expedition was dispatched. The members of the expedition were not so fortunate as to meet with the Devil. But they had obtained a lot of new information about the actions of the "unknown person" (the old scientists insisted that the word "person" should be replaced with the word "creature").

In their report published in the newspapers, the members of the expedition wrote,

6

"1. In some places on the sand bars we have noticed the tracks of narrow human feet. The tracks came from the sea and led back into the sea. However, such tracks could be left by a person coming ashore in a boat.

"2. The fishing nets we inspected bore the cuts that could be made by a very sharp instrument. It is possible that the nets got caught on sharp underground rocks or metal pieces of sunken ships and became torn.

"3. Based on the eyewitness stories, a dolphin beached by a storm and left some distance from the water was dragged into the ocean at night. The sand bore traces of feet and what appeared to be long claws. It is possible that the dolphin was rescued by some kindhearted fisherman.

"It is well known that when dolphins hunt, they help the fishermen by chasing the fish toward the sand bars. And so the fishermen frequently help dolphins in trouble. The traces of claws could have been left by human fingers, and were interpreted as claws by someone's imagination.

"4. The baby goat could have been brought over in a boat and planted by some prankster."

The scientists found other, equally simple explanations for the origins of the traces left by the Devil.

The scientists concluded that there wasn't a single sea creature that could carry out such complex actions.

Still, not everyone was satisfied by these explanations. There were those among the scientists who found the arguments questionable. How could even the most deft and persistent prankster do all these things without being seen for so long? Most importantly, the report did not include the fact that the Devil carried out his actions over short periods of time in places located far away from each other. Either the Devil could swim with incredible speed, or he had some other methods of transportation, or the Devil was not alone – there were several of them. But then, all these pranks appeared even more incomprehensible and menacing.

Pedro Zurita recalled this entire mysterious story, as he paced across his room. He didn't notice that it was morning, until a rosy beam of sunlight fell through his porthole. Pedro turned off the lamp and went to the wash basin. As he poured warm water over his head, he heard frightened cries from the deck. Abandoning his ablutions, Zurita quickly ran up the steps.

The divers clad only in loincloths were standing by the railing, waving their arms and shouting. Pedro looked down and saw that the boats left in the water overnight had been untied. The night breeze carried them fairly far into the open ocean. Now, the morning breeze was slowly taking them toward the shore. The oars were scattered all over the surface of the bay.

Zurita ordered the divers to go get the boats. But no one dared to leave the deck. Zurita repeated his order.

"You go stick your head into the Devil's claws," someone said.

Zurita put his hand on his gun holster. The divers crowded by the mast and stared at Zurita with hostility. The fight seamed unavoidable. But then Balthazar interfered.

"Arauca is afraid of no one," he said. "The shark spat me out, and the Devil too will choke on my old bones." He folded his hands above his head, dove into the water and swam toward the nearest boat.

The divers came closer to the railing and watched Balthazar fearfully. Despite his age and his wounded leg, he was an excellent swimmer. In just a few moments, the Indian reached the boat, caught an oar, and climbed in.

"The rope was cut with a knife," he shouted, "and very well cut at that! The knife had to be razor sharp."

Seeing that nothing bad happened to Balthazar, several divers followed his example.

A DOLPHIN RIDE

The sun had only been up briefly, but it was already mercilessly scorching. The silvery-blue sky was cloudless, the ocean – motionless. *Medusa* was anchored a dozen miles south of Buenos Aires. Following Balthazar's advice, they stopped in a small bay by the rocky shore rising from the water in two large shelves.

The boats were scattered through the bay. As usual, each boat had two divers – one dove, the other one pulled him up. Then they switched.

One boat came fairly close to the shore. Its diver grabbed with his feet a chunk of coral tied to a rope and quickly descended to the bottom.

The water was very warm and transparent – every stone was clearly visible. Closer to the shore, the ocean floor was covered with corals that looked like motionless trees of underwater gardens. Small fish shimmering with gold and silver darted between these "trees".

The diver reached the bottom, leaned down and started quickly gathering oyster shells and placing them into a sack tied to his belt. His partner, the Huron, held the other end of the rope in his hands, leaned over the side of the boat and watched him work.

Suddenly, the diver jumped up as quickly as he could, waved his arms, grabbed the rope and tugged it so hard that he almost pulled the Huron into the water. The boat rocked. The Huron quickly pulled up his partner and helped him climb into the boat. The diver was breathing heavily with a wide-open mouth. His eyes were bulging. His dark-bronze face looked gray from pallor.

"A shark?"

But the diver answered nothing and collapsed on the bottom of the boat.

What could have frightened him so much? The Huron leaned over and peered into the water. Yes, there was something going on there. Small fish scattered in the dense coral growth like birds at the sight of a hawk.

Suddenly, the Huron saw something like crimson smoke wafting from behind the protruding edge of an underwater rock. The smoke slowly crept in every direction, coloring the water pink. Then something dark appeared. It was a shark. It turned slowly and vanished behind the rock. The crimson smoke could only be blood spilled at the ocean floor. What happened there? The Huron looked at his partner, but he still lay on his back, gasping for air and gazing vacantly at the sky. The Indian grabbed the oars and hurried to take his suddenly ill friend to *Medusa*.

The diver finally recovered, but he seemed to have gone mute – he just kept humming, shaking his head and gasping with his lips pouting.

The divers still aboard the schooner surrounded him, impatiently waiting for an explanation.

"Speak!" a young Indian finally said and shook the diver. "Speak if you don't want your cowardly soul to be knocked right out of your body."

The diver shook his head once again and said in a dull voice, "I saw… the Sea Devil."

"Really?"

"Come on, tell us, tell us!" the divers shouted.

"I saw the shark. The shark was coming right at me. I thought it was the end! Big, black, mouth wide open – all ready to gobble me up. Then I saw something else…"

"Another shark?"

"The Devil!"

"What was he like? Did he have a head?"

"A head? Yes, I think. Huge eyes."

"If he has eyes, then he must have a head," the young Indian stated confidently. "The eyes have to be nailed down to something. Did he have hands?"

"He had paws, like a frog's. Long fingers, green, with talons and webbing. He was all shiny, like a fish in its scales. He swam up to the shark, raised one paw – swish! Blood from the shark's belly…"

"What kind of legs did he have?" another diver asked.

"Legs?" the diver tried remembering. "There were no legs. A big tail. And two snakes at the end of it."

"What scared you more – the shark or the monster?"

"The monster," he replied without hesitation. "The monster, even though he saved my life. It was *him*…"

"Yes, had to be him."

"The Sea Devil," the Indian said.

"Or the Sea God who comes to help the poor," an old Indian corrected. This news quickly spread through other boats in the bay. The divers rushed to the schooner and raised the boats out of the water.

10

Everyone surrounded the diver saved by the Sea Devil. He said that there were red flames coming out of the monster's nose, and his teeth were sharp and as long as one's fingers. His ears moved, there were fins on his sides, and his tail was the size of an oar.

Pedro Zurita dressed in short white pants, sandals, and a tall wide straw hat paced around the deck and listened in on the conversation.

The more the storyteller got carried away, the more Pedro became convinced that this was all made up by the diver, frightened by the approaching shark.

"Although, it might not all be lies. Someone did slice that shark open – the water in the bay turned pink. The Indian is lying, but there is a shred of truth in this. Damn, what a strange story!"

Zurita's thoughts were interrupted by a trumpet sound from behind the nearest rock.

The sound struck *Medusa*'s crew like thunder. All conversation stopped immediately, everyone went pale. The divers gazed at the rock with superstitious dread.

There was a group of dolphins playing near the surface not far from the rock. One of the dolphins separated from the group, snorted loudly, as if responding to the call of the trumpet, swam quickly to the rock and vanished. A few more seconds of strained waiting passed. Suddenly the divers saw the dolphin coming back. On his back rode a strange creature – the Devil the rescued diver spoke about. The monster had a human body. On his face were enormous eyes, the size of old-fashioned pocket watches, gleaming in the sun like car headlights. His skin shimmered with delicate blue silver, and his hands looked like a frog's – they were webbed, dark green, with long fingers. His legs below the knee were in the water. It was impossible to tell whether they ended in a tail or they were ordinary human legs. The strange creature held a spiral seashell in his hand. Once again, he made the trumpet sound with the shell, laughed with a merry human laughter, and then shouted in perfect Spanish, "Come on, Leading, move!" He patted the dolphin's glistening back with his frog hand and squeezed the dolphin's sides with his knees. Like a well-trained horse, the dolphin put on speed.

The divers shrieked.

The unusual rider glanced back. When he saw the people watching him, he slipped off the dolphin's back, as quick as a lizard, and hid behind him. A green hand appeared from behind the dolphin, patting the animal on the back. The obedient dolphin submerged along with the monster.

The strange pair made a half circle underwater and vanished behind a rock.

This unusual ride took no more than a minute, but the spectators couldn't recover from astonishment for a long time.

The divers screamed, ran around the deck, and grabbed their heads. Some of the Indians fell to their knees and begged the sea gods to spare them. A young Mexican climbed the main mast and kept screaming. A couple of Negros stumbled down into the hold and hid there.

The diving was out of the question. Pedro and Balthazar barely managed to restore order. *Medusa* raised anchor and headed north.

ZURITA'S FAILURE

The captain of Medusa went below deck to think about what happened.

"This is crazy!" Zurita said, pouring a pitcher of warm water over his head. "The sea monster speaks perfect Castillo dialect! What is this? Sorcery? Madness? But the entire crew can't go mad all at once. Even two people can't have the same dream at the same time. We have all seen the Sea Devil. Without a question. Which means he exists, as impossible as it may seem."

Zurita poured more water on his head and looked out the porthole for some fresh air.

"Regardless," he continued, having calmed down somewhat, "this monstrous creature has human intelligence and can carry out intelligent actions. He clearly feels equally well in water and out of it. And he speaks Spanish, which means one can reach an understanding with him. And what if... What if I could catch this monster, tame it, and make it get pearls for me! This frog capable of living in the water can replace an entire crew of divers. And the profits! Every pearl diver has to be paid a quarter of his daily catch. And this frog would cost me nothing. I could make hundreds of thousands, even millions in a short time!"

Zurita became lost in his dreams. Until then, he was hoping to make his fortune by looking for pearls where no one tried before. Persian Gulf, the western shore of Ceylon, the Red Sea, Australia – all these pearl troves were far away, and people had been gathering pearls there for a long time. Should he sail to the Mexican or California Gulfs? To the islands of Thomas and Margarita? Zurita could not go to the shores of Venezuela, known for the best pearls in the Americas. His schooner was too dilapidated for that, and he didn't have enough divers – in other words, he first had to expand his business. Zurita did not have enough money. And so he was stuck by the shores of Argentina. But now! Now he could get rich in one year, if only he could catch the Sea Devil.

He would become the wealthiest man in Argentina, perhaps even in America. Money would pave his road to power. Pedro Zurita's name would become famous. But he had to be very careful. First and foremost, he should keep his plans secret.

Zurita went above deck, gathered the entire crew, including the cook, and said, "Do you know what happened to everyone who spread rumors about the Sea Devil? They were arrested and put into prison. I must warn you that this is what will happen to any of you who mentions having seen the Sea Devil. You will rot in jail. Understand? If you value your life – not a word about the Devil."

"No one will believe them anyway – this all sounds too much like a fairy tale," Zurita thought and, inviting Balthazar into his room, told him about his plan.

Balthazar carefully listened to the captain and replied after a pause, "Yes, this is good. The Sea Devil is worth a hundred divers. It would be good to have the Devil in your service. But how are we to catch him?"

"With a net," Zurita replied.

"He will cut the net the way he sliced through the shark's belly."

"We can order a metal net."

"Who will catch him? Try telling our divers, 'Go catch the Devil,' and their knees start shaking. They won't agree even for a sack of gold."

"What about you, Balthazar?"

The Indian shrugged, "I have never hunted sea devils before. It won't be easy to ambush him, but not so hard to kill him, if he is made of meat and bones. But you want the live Devil."

"You aren't afraid of him, Balthazar, are you? What do you think of the Sea Devil?"

"What can I think about a jaguar flying over the ocean or a shark climbing trees? An unknown beast is always frightening. But I do like hunting scary beasts."

"I shall reward you generously." Zurita shook Balthazar's hand and continued outlining his plan, "The fewer people participate in this the better. Talk to your Arauca people. They are brave and clever. Pick five men, no more. If none of our people agree, find some on the side. The Devil sticks to the shoreline. First, we must track down where his den is. After that, catching him should be easy."

Zurita and Balthazar quickly went to work. Zurita ordered wire cage that looked like a large barrel without a bottom. Inside, Zurita suspended rope nets so that the Devil would get tangled in them, like in a spider web. The divers were let go. Of the entire *Medusa* crew, Balthazar managed to convince only two Arauca to participate in the hunt for the Devil. He hired three more in Buenos Aires.

They decided to start tracking the Devil in the same bay where Medusa's crew first saw him. To keep from spooking the Devil *Medusa* dropped anchor a few miles away from the original spot. Zurita and his companions spent some time fishing as if that was the original purpose of their trip. At the same time, three of them took turns hiding behind the rocks on the shore and watching what was happening in the water.

At the end of the second week, there was still no sign of the Devil.

Balthazar struck up conversations with the local villagers and Indian farmers, selling them cheap fish and talking to them about different things, subtly steering the conversation toward the Sea Devil. Based on these talks, the old Indian found out that they picked the right spot for their hunt – many Indians living by the bay had heard the trumpet sound and seen the tracks on the sand. They stated that the Devil's heels were human, but his toes were significantly longer. Sometimes the Indians noticed an imprint of a back on the sand where he rested.

The Devil caused no harm to the locals, and they stopped paying attention to the tracks he left from time to time. But they had never seen the Devil himself.

Medusa stayed in the bay for two weeks, supposedly for fishing. For two weeks Zurita, Balthazar, and the hired Indians kept an eye on the surface of the ocean, but the Sea Devil did not appear. Zurita was becoming restless. He was impatient and stingy. Every day cost him money, and the Devil kept them waiting. Pedro was beginning to have doubts. If the Devil was a supernatural creature, he could not be captured with nets. Besides, it could be dangerous – Pedro was superstitious. Should he have invited a priest to *Medusa*, with his cross and holy water? That would mean more expenses. What if the Sea Devil was not a devil at all, but some prankster – a good swimmer who dressed as the Devil to frighten people? What about the dolphin? Like any other animal, he could be tamed and trained. Should they abandon this entire idea?

Zurita promised a reward to anyone who first noticed the Devil and decided to wait a few more days.

To his joy, at the beginning of the third week, the Devil made a few appearances.

After the day's fishing Balthazar left the boat filled with fish by the shore. In the morning, he would meet with the buyers.

15

Balthazar then went to a farm to visit a friend, but when he returned, the boat was empty. Balthazar immediately decided it had to be the Devil.

"Did he really eat all this fish?" Balthazar wondered.

The same night, one of the Indians keeping watch heard the trumpet sound to the south from the bay. Two days later, in the morning, one of the young Arauca informed that he finally managed to track down the Devil. He arrived with the dolphin. This time, the Devil was not riding the dolphin, but swimming next to it, holding on to the "harness" – a wide leather collar. In the bay, the Devil took the collar off the dolphin, patted the animal, and vanished in the back of the bay, at the foot of a sheer drop. The dolphin surfaced and then vanished.

Zurita listened to the Arauca, thanked him, promised a reward and said, "The Devil is unlikely to leave his den today. We should examine the bottom of the bay. Who will do it?"

But no one wanted to go to the ocean floor and risk meeting the unknown monster face-to-face.

Balthazar stepped forward.

"Here I am!" he said. Balthazar was true to his work. Medusa was still anchored. Everyone but the watchmen went to the shore and walked to the sheer drop by the bay. Balthazar tied a rope around his waist, so that someone could pull him up, should he be wounded, took a knife, wrapped his legs around a rock and dropped to the bottom.

The Arauca impatiently waiting for his return peered at the spot flickering in the bluish gloom of the bay, overshadowed by the rocks. Forty seconds passed, fifty, a minute – Balthazar was not back. Finally he pulled on the rope and they lifted him to the surface. Having caught his breath, Balthazar said, "There is a narrow passageway leading into an underground cave. It's as dark as inside of a shark's belly. The Sea Devil could only have gone into that cave. There is a solid rock wall around it."

"Excellent!" Zurita exclaimed. "The darker the better! We shall set up our nets and catch our little fish."

Shortly after sunset, the Indians lowered the wire nets attached to strong ropes across the cave entrance. The ends of the ropes were fastened to posts on the shore. Balthazar tied bells to the ropes to make them ring the moment the nets were touched.

Zurita, Balthazar and five Arauca sat down on the beach and waited.

16

No one was left on the schooner.

Darkness fell quickly. The moon rose and its light reflected in the surface of the ocean. Everyone became unusually agitated. Perhaps they were about to see the strange creature that struck such terror in the hearts of fishermen and pearl divers.

The hours passed slowly. People started dozing off.

Suddenly the bells rang. People jumped up, ran to the ropes, and started pulling up the net. It was heavy. The ropes shook. Someone was struggling inside the net.

Finally the net surfaced, and in the pale moonlight they saw a half-man/half-beast thrashing in the net. His enormous eyes and silvery scales sparkled. The Devil was making incredible efforts to free a hand tangled in the net. He finally succeeded. He pulled out a knife hanging on a slender strap at his hip and started cutting the net.

"Oh no, you don't," Balthazar said quietly, absorbed in the hunt.

Much to his surprise, the knife managed to overcome the wire. With a few deft movements the Devil widened the hole, and the divers rushed to pull the net to the shore.

"Pull harder! Come on!" Balthazar shouted.

Just when their prey seemed to be in their hands, the Devil fell through the hole he made, fell into the water raising a fountain of sparkling water drops, and vanished in the depth.

The divers dropped the net in dismay.

"What a great knife! It cuts through the wire!" Balthazar said appreciatively. "The underwater blacksmiths must be better than ours."

Zurita lowered his head and stared at the water as if his entire fortune had just sunk in there.

He then looked up, tugged on his bushy mustache and stomped his foot.

"No, no way!" he shouted. "You would sooner die in your underwater cave than I give up. I won't spare any money, I shall hire scuba divers, I will cover the entire bay with nets and traps, but you won't get away from me!"

He was brave, persistent, and stubborn. There was a reason the blood of Spanish conquistadors flowed in Pedro Zurita's veins. Besides, this was worth fighting for.

The Sea Devil was not a supernatural omnipotent creature after all. He was clearly made of "meat and bones" as Balthazar said. Which meant he could be caught, chained, and forced to get the riches for Zurita from the ocean floor. Balthazar would get him, even if Neptune himself came to defend the Sea Devil with his trident.

Zurita carried out his threat. He installed many wire barriers at the bottom of the bay, stretched nets in every direction, and placed many traps. But so far, he caught nothing but fish, and the Sea Devil seemed to have vanished into thin air. He did not appear anymore and gave no signs of his presence. His pet dolphin appeared every day in vain, diving and snorting, as if inviting his unusual friend to go for a ride. No one showed up, and the dolphin gave one final frustrated snort and left for the open sea.

The weather was getting worse. Wind blowing from the east rippled the surface of the ocean; the waters of the bay turned turbid from the sand rising from the bottom. Foaming wave crests concealed the ocean floor. No one could tell what was going on underwater.

Zurita stood on the shore for hours, gazing at the rows of waves. Enormous, they came one after another, crashing in loud waterfalls, as the lower layers of water rolled further across the damp sand, hissing, carrying pebbles and seashells, and almost reaching Zurita's feet.

"No, this is not going to work," Zurita said. "I have to come up with something else. The Devil lives at the bottom of the sea and doesn't wish to come out of his den. Which means, in order to catch him, we must go to him on the ocean floor. That much is clear!"

Zurita turned to Balthazar who was making yet another complex trap and said, "Go to Buenos Aires and bring two diving suits with oxygen tanks. The ordinary suit with a hose for pumping the air won't do. The Devil might cut the hose. Besides, we may have to go on a little underwater walk. And don't forget to get powerful electric flashlights."

"Do you wish to go visit the Devil?" Balthazar asked.

"With you of course, old man." Balthazar nodded and set out. He not only brought the suits and the lights, but also a couple of long fancifully curving bronze knives.

"They don't make them like that anymore," he said. "These are the ancient Arauca knives my great-grandfathers used to cut up your white great-grandfathers, no offense."

Zurita didn't like this historic reference, but he did approve of the knives.

"You are very prudent, Balthazar."

The next day, at dawn, despite the waves, Zurita and Balthazar put on their diving gear and descended to the ocean floor. Not without some difficulty they untangled the nets blocking the entrance to the underwater cavern and crawled into the narrow passage. They were in complete darkness. Once they gained their footing and pulled out their knives, the divers turned on their flashlights. Frightened by the light, small fish darted off to the side, but then returned to it, crowding in the bluish beam like a swarm of insects.

Zurita brushed them off with his hand – their sparkling scales blinded him. This was a fairly large cave, no less than twelve feet high and fifteen to twenty feet wide. The divers examined the nooks and crannies of the cave. It was empty and uninhabited save for the schools of small fish hiding here from the storm and predators.

Stepping carefully, Zurita and Balthazar moved forward. The cave gradually narrowed. Suddenly, Zurita halted in astonishment. The light from his lamp fell onto a thick metal grate obstructing their path.

Zurita could not believe his eyes. He grabbed the metal bars and started shaking them, hoping to open the barrier. But the grate didn't move. Moving his flashlight closer, Zurita discovered that the grate was securely set into the cave's roughly hewed walls, and had hinges and an internal lock.

This was a new riddle.

The Sea Devil was not only intelligent but an exceptionally gifted creature.

He tamed the dolphin and knew metallurgy. The last but not the least, he could make strong metal barriers at the bottom of the sea to protect his dwelling. But this was impossible! He couldn't have very well forged steel underwater. …Which meant he didn't live in the water or, at the very least, he briefly came out to the surface.

Zurita felt a thrumming in his temples, as if there was not enough oxygen in his diving helmet, even though he had only spent a few minutes underwater.

Zurita gestured to Balthazar and they left the underwater cavern. There was nothing left to do there, and they returned to the surface.

The Arauca waited for them anxiously and were very glad to see the divers return unharmed.

Having taken off his helmet and caught his breath, Zurita asked, "What do you think, Balthazar?"

The Indian spread his hands.

"All I can say is that we would have to wait here for a long time. The Devil must eat fish, and there is plenty of fish there. We can't lure him out of the cave by hunger. All we can do is blow up the grate with dynamite."

"Do you suppose, Balthazar, that the cave might have two exits – one into the bay, and another one on the surface?"

Balthazar hasn't thought of that.

"You would think so. Why didn't we try checking out the surroundings?" Zurita said.

They started examining the shoreline.

Zurita stumbled onto a tall wall of white stone, surrounding a huge plot of land – no less than twenty-five acres. Zurita followed the wall. He found only one set of gates made of heavy iron sheets. In the gates was a small metal door with a peephole covered from the inside.

"It's a real prison or fortress," Zurita thought. "Strange! Farmers don't build such thick and tall walls. There isn't a single gap or crack in the wall, no way to look inside."

Around him all was wild and deserted – bare gray rocks with thorny brush and cacti growing here and there. Below him was the bay.

Zurita walked along the wall for several days and watched the gates. But they never opened, and no one entered or came out. Not a single sound came from beyond the wall.

Having returned to Medusa in the evening, Zurita met with Balthazar and asked, "Do you know who lives in the fortress above the bay?"

"I do, I have already asked the Indians working at the farms. Salvator lives there."

"Who is he, this Salvator?"

"God," Balthazar replied.

Zurita raised his thick black eyebrows in surprise.

"Are you joking, Balthazar?"

The Indian smiled slightly, "I am only repeating what I heard. Many Indians call Salvator a god and a savior."

"What does he save them from?"

"Death. They say he is omnipotent. Salvator can do miracles. He holds life and death in his hands. He gives the lame new legs to walk on,

21

the blind – new eyes as keen as an eagle's, and even resurrects the dead."

"Damn!" Zurita cursed, fluffing his mustache. "There is the Sea Devil in the bay and a god living above it. Do you suppose, Balthazar, that those two might be helping each other?"

"I suppose that we should get out of here as soon as possible, before our brains curdle like sour milk from all these wonders."

"Have you seen any of those cured by Salvator?"

"Yes, I have. I saw a man with a broken leg. Having visited Salvator, this man runs like a mustang. I also saw an Indian who was resurrected by Salvator. The entire village said that when they carried him to Salvator, this man was a corpse – with a cracked skull and his brains spilling out. But he returned from Salvator alive and happy. Got married after his 'death'. To a nice girl. I also saw their children."

"Then Salvator does receive visitors?"

"Only Indians. And they come to him from everywhere – from Tierra del Fuego and the Amazon, from the desert of Atacama and Asuncion."

Having received this information from Balthazar, Zurita decided to go to Buenos Aires.

There he found out that Salvator treated Indians and had a reputation of a miracle worker among them. Zurita consulted a group of doctors and discovered that Salvator was a talented, even brilliant surgeon, but a man of great eccentricity like many geniuses. Salvator's name was well known in the scientific circles of the Old and the New World. In America, he became famous for his bold surgeries. When the patients' condition was considered hopeless and other doctors refused to operate, Salvator was called upon. He never refused. His bravery and ingenuity were without limits. During World War I he served as an army surgeon at the French Front, where he engaged almost exclusively in cranial operations. Thousands of people owed him their lives. After the war ended, he went home, to Argentina. His medical practice and successful real estate deals secured Salvator's enormous fortune. He bought a large plot of land near Buenos Aires, surrounded it by a tall wall – one of his eccentricities – moved in, and stopped practicing medicine entirely. He engaged only in scientific work at his private laboratory. Presently, he resumed his practice but received and treated only Indians, who called him a god who came to earth to protect them.

Zurita managed to discover another detail pertaining to Salvator's past. Before the war, there used to be a modest house with a garden, also surrounded by a wall, where Salvator's vast property was presently located. The house was guarded by a Negro and several huge dogs. These faithful sentinels didn't allow a single person beyond the gates.

Lately, Salvator surrounded himself with an even greater mystery. He didn't receive even his former friends from the university.

Having found out all this, Zurita decided, "If Salvator is a doctor, he has no right to refuse a patient. Why can't I become ill? I can come to see Salvator as a patient, and then we'll see."

Zurita went to the iron gates blocking the entrance to Salvator's domain and started knocking. He knocked for a long time, but no one opened. Enraged, Zurita picked up a large rock and started slamming it against the gates, making enough noise to raise the dead.

Dogs barked somewhere in the distance, and finally the peephole in the door opened.

"What do you want?" someone said in broken Spanish.

"A patient, open up quickly," Zurita replied.

"Patients don't knock like that," the same voice replied calmly, and someone's eyes appeared in the peephole. "The doctor is not receiving today."

"He can't refuse helping a patient," Zurita was losing his temper.

The peephole closed, and someone's footsteps faded in the distance. Only the dogs kept barking at the top of their lungs.

Having exhausted his vocabulary of cusswords, Zurita returned to the schooner. Should he complain about Salvator in Buenos Aires? Bit this wouldn't help. Zurita was shaking with anger. His bushy black mustache was in serious danger, because he kept tugging at it constantly in his agitation, and it drooped like a barometer showing low atmospheric pressure.

Gradually, he calmed down and started thinking what to do next.

As he pondered, his tanned fingers kept fluffing his mustache up. The barometer was rising.

Finally he came above deck and suddenly gave an order to sail.

Medusa was returning to Buenos Aires.

"Very well," Balthazar said. "So much time wasted! To hell with the Devil and his pal the god!"

THE SICK GRANDDAUGHTER

The sun was scorching.

An old, exhausted Indian was walking down the dusty road between the fertile wheat, corn and oat fields. His clothes were torn. In his arms he carried a sick child, covered from the sun with a threadbare blanket. The child's eyes were half-closed. There was a large swelling on her neck. From time to time, when the old man stumbled, the child moaned hoarsely and opened her eyes. The old man paused and blew into the child's face to cool her down.

"I hope she makes it there alive!" the old man whispered, walking faster.

Having reached the iron gates, the Indian transferred the child into his left arm, and knocked four times with his right fist. The peephole opened, someone's eye looked through briefly, then the bars screeched and the door opened.

The Indian timidly stepped over the threshold. Before him stood an old Negro with completely white curly hair, dressed in a white coat.

"I am here to see the doctor, my granddaughter is sick," the Indian said.

The Negro nodded silently, locked the door and gestured for him to follow.

The Indian looked around. They were in a small courtyard paved with large stone tiles. On one side the courtyard was surrounded by the tall outside wall, on the other – by a lower wall separating the courtyard from the rest of the property. There wasn't a single blade of grass or even a small shrub – it looked like a prison yard. In the corner of the courtyard by the gates in the second wall there was a large white building with wide windows. On the ground by the building sat the Indians – men and women. Many were with children.

Almost all of the children looked perfectly healthy. Some were playing "even and odd" with seashells, others wrestled silently – the old Negro with white hair watched them carefully to make sure they didn't make much noise.

The old Indian obediently settled onto the ground in the shadow of the building and started blowing into the child's still, bluish face. Next to him sat an old woman with a swollen leg. She glanced at the child in the Indian's lap and asked, "Your daughter?"

"Granddaughter," the Indian replied. The old woman shook her head and said, "The swamp spirit possessed your daughter. But *he* is stronger than the evil spirits. *He* will chase away the swamp spirit, and your granddaughter will be well."

The Indian nodded.

The Negro in the white coat passed along the line of patients, looked at the Indian's child and pointed at the door of the building.

The Indian entered a large room with stone tiled floor. Another door opened – this one with frosted glass – and Doctor Salvator entered. He was tall, swarthy, broad-shouldered, and also wore a white coat. Aside from black eyebrows and eyelashes, there wasn't a single hair on Salvator's head. He must have shaved his head regularly, because the skin on his head was as tanned as his face. He had a large aquiline nose, somewhat protruding pointed chin, and firmly pressed lips, which gave his face a cruel and even predatory expression. His brown eyes were cold. The Indian felt awkward under his gaze.

The Indian bowed and held out the child. Salvator took the sick girl from the Indian's arm in one swift, confident, but also careful movement, unwrapped the rags she was wrapped in and threw them into the corner of the room, deftly hitting the trash box. The Indian clambered toward the box to retrieve the rags, but Salvator stopped him sternly, "Leave it, don't touch!"

He then placed the girl on the table and leaned over her. The Indian saw his profile. He suddenly imagined that this wasn't a doctor, but a condor crouching over a little bird. Salvator started touching the swelling on the child's throat. The Indian was struck by his fingers. They were long and uncommonly agile. They seemed to bend not only down but sideways or even up. The Indian was not a timid man, but he struggled not to fall prey to the dread inspired by this strange man.

"Beautiful. Splendid," Salvator said, seemingly admiring the swelling as he examined it.

Having finished with the patient, Salvator looked at the Indian and said, "It's new moon now. Come in a month, the next new moon, and you will get your little girl back in good health."

He took the child behind the glass door, where the bathroom, the surgery, and the patient rooms were located. The Negro was already showing in the next patient – the old woman with the swollen leg.

The Indian bowed to the glass door that closed behind Salvator and left.

Exactly twenty-eight days later the same glass door opened.

In the doorway stood the little girl, healthy and glowing, wearing a new dress. She gave her grandfather a furtive glance. The Indian ran to her, swept her up, kissed her and examined her throat. There wasn't a trace of the swelling. Only a small, barely noticeable red scar reminded of the operation.

The girl pushed her grandfather away and even shrieked when he kissed her and prickled her with the stubble on his unshaved chin. He had to set her down. Salvator entered after the girl. The doctor smiled, patted the girl on the head, and said, "Here is your little girl back. You brought her to me in time. A few more hours, and even I couldn't have brought her back to life."

The old Indian's face creased, his lips shook, and tears flowed from his eyes. He once again picked up the girl, clasped her to his chest, fell to his knees before Salvator, and said in a halting voice, "You saved my granddaughter's life, sir. What can a poor Indian offer you in return, except for his life?"

"What do I need your life for?" Salvator asked in surprise.

"I am old, but I am still strong," the Indian continued, still kneeling. "I shall take my granddaughter to her mother – my daughter – and return to you. I wish to dedicate the rest of my life to you, for the kindness you did me. I shall serve you like a dog. Please, do not deny me this favor."

Salvator pondered.

He hired new staff very reluctantly and carefully, even though there was work to do. Indeed, there was plenty of work – Jim was barely managing in the garden. This Indian looked like a suitable man, although the doctor would have preferred a Negro.

"You are giving me your life and asking me to accept your gift, as a favor. Very well. Have it your way. When can you be back?"

"I shall be here before the first quarter of the new moon," the Indian said, kissing the hem of Salvator's white coat.

"What is your name?"

"My name? Christo. Christopher."

"Go, Christo. I shall wait for you."

"Come along, girl!" Christo told his granddaughter and picked her up.

The little girl cried. Christo hurried to leave.

THE GARDEN OF WONDERS

When Christo returned a week later, Doctor Salvator thoughtfully looked him in the eye and said, "Listen carefully, Christo. I am going to hire you. You will have room, board, and a good salary…"

Christo waved his hands, "I don't need anything, I just want to serve you."

"Be quiet and listen," Salvator continued. "You will have everything you need. But I require one thing – you must keep quiet about everything you see here."

"I would sooner cut off my tongue and throw it to the dogs than say a single word."

"Make sure this doesn't happen to you," Salvator warned. He called the Negro in the white coat and ordered, "Take him to the garden and introduce him to Jim."

The Negro bowed, led the Indian out of the white building, took him across the courtyard and knocked on the iron door in the second wall.

Dogs barking sounded from behind the wall, the door creaked and slowly opened.

The Negro pushed Christo through the door into the garden, shouted something to another man and left.

Christo backed up against the wall in fright – strange reddish-yellow animals with dark spots were running at him, barking and roaring at the same time. Had Christo met them in the pampas he would have recognized them as jaguars. But these animals were barking like dogs. Presently, Christo didn't care what kind of animals attacked him. He ran to the nearest tree and started climbing its branches with unexpected speed. Another Negro appeared and hissed at the dogs, like an angry cobra. They instantly calmed down. They stopped barking, settled down on the ground, and rested their heads on their outstretched paws, casting an occasional glance at the man who subdued them.

The Negro hissed again, this time addressing Christo, who was sitting in the tree. He gestured, inviting the Indian to climb down.

"Why are you hissing like a snake?" Christo said, refusing to leave his perch. "Cat got your tongue?" The Negro hummed indignantly.

"Maybe he is a mute," Christo thought and remembered Salvator's warning. Did Salvator really cut off his servants' tongues for betraying his secrets? Perhaps, this man's tongue has been cut out. Christo suddenly

felt so frightened that he nearly fell off the tree. He wanted to run away from here no matter what and as quickly as possible. He mentally checked how far his tree was from the wall. No, it was too far to jump. The Negro walked up to the tree, grabbed the Indian's foot and impatiently pulled him down. He had to cooperate. Christo jumped down, smiled as friendly as he could, held out his hand and asked pleasantly, "Jim?"

The Negro nodded.

Christo shook his hand. *"If I am in hell, I might as well get along with the demons,"* he thought, then continued out loud, "Are you a mute?" The Negro did not reply.

"Don't you have a tongue?"

The man still remained silent.

"How do I get a look into his mouth?" Christo thought. But Jim clearly had no intention of striking up a conversation, even with signs and gestures. He took Christo's hand, led him to the reddish-yellow animals and hissed at them. The animals rose, walked up to Christo, sniffed him, then calmly walked away. Christo felt a little better.

Jim gestured to invite Christo for a tour of the house.

After the dull stone courtyard the garden astonished with its luxuriant greenery and abundance of flowers. The garden stretched to the east, gradually sloping toward the ocean. The paths covered with reddish ground-up seashells ran in every direction. Next to the paths grew the fanciful cacti, bluish-green juicy agaves, and reeds with a multitude of brush-like yellow-green flowers. Entire groves of peach and olive trees cast shadows over thick grass scattered with bright, colorful flowers. Amidst the greenery sparkled pools of water encased in white stone. Tall fountains cooled the air.

The garden was filled with various shouts, singing, and twittering of birds, roaring, screeching, and squealing of animals. Christo has never seen such strange beasts. This garden was inhabited by some wondrous creatures.

A six-legged lizard ran across their path, its coppery-green scale gleaming in the sun. A two-headed snake hung from a tree. Christo was startled by it and staggered away from the two-headed reptile hissing at him with two red mouths. The Negro responded with an even louder hiss, and the snake swung its two heads, dropped from the tree and vanished in a dense cluster of reeds. Another long snake crawled away from the

29

path, propelling itself on two paws. A piglet grunted at them from behind a wire net. It stared at Christo with a large solitary eye in the middle of its forehead.

Two white rats merged at the side were running down the pink path, like a kind of two-headed, eight-legged monster. Sometimes, this creature tried fighting with itself – the right rat pulling to the right, and the left one – to the left, with both of them squeaking angrily. The right one always won. Another pair of "Siamese twins" – two merino sheep – were grazing near the path. They were not fighting like the rats. Apparently, they had long since established a unity of wills and desires. Another freak made a particular impression upon Christo – a large, completely hairless, pink dog. On its back, seemingly growing out of the dog's body, was a small monkey – its chest, hands, and head. The dog walked up to Christo and wagged its tail. The monkey looked around, waved its arms, patted the back of the dog, with which it was merged and shouted, looking at Christo. The Indian put his hand into his pocket, pulled out a piece of sugar and held it out to the monkey. But someone quickly pushed away his hand. He heard hissing. Christo looked back at Jim. The Negro gestured at Christo, indicating that he should not feed the monkey. Instantly, a sparrow with the head of a small parrot dove down, pulled the sugar out of Christo's hands and vanished behind a bush. A horse with a cow's head mooed in a distant clearing.

Two llamas ran across the clearing, swishing their equine tales. Unusual reptiles, animals, and birds stared at Christo from the grass, from the thick brush, and from tree branches – dogs with feline heads, geese with the heads of roosters, horned boars, ostriches with eagle beaks, sheep with the body of a puma.

Christo felt as if he was delirious. He rubbed his eyes, stuck his head under the cold water of the fountains, but nothing helped. In the pools he saw snakes with fish heads and gills, fishes with frog legs, and enormous toads with elongated lizard bodies.

Once again Christo felt the urge to run away.

Finally, Jim took Christo to a wide clearing covered with sand. In the middle of the clearing, surrounded with palm trees, stood a white marble villa built in the Mauritanian style. Between the palm trunks he could see arches and columns. Copper fountains in the shape of dolphins spilled cascades of water into crystal-clear pools with playful goldfish. The largest fountain in front of the main entrance portrayed a young man riding a dolphin, akin to the mythical Triton, with a spiral seashell at his lips.

Behind the villa were several cottages and shops, followed by a dense cluster of cacti reaching all the way to the white wall.

"Another wall!" Christo thought.

Jim led the Indian into a modest cool room. He gestured to indicate that this room belonged to him and walked out, leaving Christo alone.

THE THIRD WALL

Gradually, Christo became accustomed to the unusual world that surrounded him. All of the animals, birds, and reptiles living in the garden were tame. Christo even became friends with some of them. The jaguar-colored dogs that frightened him so much on his first day, now followed him everywhere, licked his hands, and asked to be petted. The llamas accepted pieces of bread from his hands. The parrots fluttered down to sit on his shoulder.

Twelve servants took care of the garden and the animals, all of them as quiet or mute as Jim. Christo never heard them talk even to each other. Each one attended to his job in silence. Jim was a kind of overseer. He watched the others and assigned their duties. Christo, much to his surprise, was appointed as Jim's assistant. Christo didn't have all that much work, and the food was good. He had nothing to complain about. One thing bothered him – the sinister silence of the black servants. He was certain that Salvator had cut out their tongues. When Salvator ordered Christo to his office from time to time, the Indian always thought, *"He is going to cut off my tongue."* But eventually, Christo stopped worrying about the fate of his tongue.

One time, Christo saw Jim sleeping in the shadow of the olive trees. The Negro rested on his back with his mouth open. Christo took this opportunity, carefully peeked into the sleeping man's mouth, and ascertained that the old Negro's tongue was in place. The Indian finally calmed down.

Salvator's day was rigidly scheduled. From seven to nine in the morning he received his Indian patients, from nine to eleven he was in surgery, and then he went into his villa and worked in the laboratory. He operated on animals, and then studied them. When his observations were finished, Salvator released these animals into the garden. From time to time, when Christo was cleaning at the house, he snuck into the laboratory. Everything he saw there astonished him. Various organs pulsed in glass jars filled with mysterious solutions. Cut-off arms and legs continued to live. When these living body parts got sick, Salvator treated them, restoring their fading life.

All this terrified Christo. He preferred being among the living monsters in the garden.

Despite the trust Salvator bestowed upon the Indian, Christo did not dare to make an attempt to get behind the third wall. But he was very interested in it. One afternoon, when everyone was resting, Christo ran up to the tall wall. He heard children's voices and was able to distinguish a few Indian words. But sometimes, the children's voices were joined by someone else's more shrill, squealing voices, as if arguing with them and speaking in an unknown dialect.

Once, having met Christo in the garden, Salvator walked up to him and said, looking him straight in the eye as usual, "You have been working for me for a month, Christo, and I am pleased with your work. One of my servants from the lower garden has fallen ill. You shall replace him. You will see many new things there. But remember our agreement – hold your tongue if you don't want to lose it."

"I have almost forgotten how to speak what with your mute servants, sir," Christo replied.

"All the better. Silence is golden. If you keep quiet, you shall receive many golden pesos. I am hoping to have my sick servant back on his feet in two weeks. By the way, how well do you know the Andes?"

"I was born in the mountains."

"Splendid. I need new animals and birds for my zoo. I shall take you with me. You may go now. Jim will take you to the lower garden."

Christo was used to many things by now. But what he saw in the lower garden surpassed his expectations.

He saw naked children and monkeys playing in a large sunlit meadow. The children were from various Indian tribes. Some of them were very young – no more than three years of age. The oldest of them were no more than twelve. These children were Salvator's patients. Many of them had been through serious surgeries and owed Salvator their lives. The recovering children played and ran around the garden, and once they had regained their strength, their parents could take them home.

The monkeys resided side-by-side with the children. They were monkeys without tails. In fact, they didn't have a scrap of fur on their bodies.

The most amazing thing was that all of the monkeys could talk, although some of them better than others. They argued with the children, shouted, and screeched in their high-pitched voices. Still, the monkeys co-existed with the children fairly peacefully and fought with them no more than the children fought amongst themselves.

Christo could not decide whether these were real monkeys or some strange class of people.

When Christo became familiar with the layout of the garden, he noticed that it was smaller than the other one, and sloped toward the bay at an even steeper angle, ending in a sheer rock wall.

The sea had to be directly behind the rock. He could hear the sound of the surf from beyond.

Having examined this wall for a few days, Christo discovered that it was artificial. Behind a thicket of wisterias Christo discovered a gray metal door, painted to match the rocks and almost completely unnoticeable.

Christo listened. Not a single sound could be heard from behind the rock wall, other than the surf. Where did this narrow door lead? To the beach?

Suddenly, he heard an excited shout of a child. The children were looking up. Christo looked up as well and saw a red balloon slowly flying across the garden. The wind was carrying the balloon off toward the sea.

The ordinary balloon flying over the garden agitated Christo greatly. He became restless. As soon as the lower garden servant recovered and returned, Christo went to Salvator and told him, "Doctor! We are getting ready to go to the Andes, perhaps, for a long time. Let me go see my daughter and granddaughter."

Salvator didn't like it when his servants left the premises and preferred to hire unattached men. Christo waited, gazing into Salvator's eyes.

Salvator looked at Christo coldly and reminded him, "Remember our agreement. Hold your tongue! Come back no later than in three days. Wait!"

Salvator went to another room and came back with a suede pouch with gold pesos.

"This is for your granddaughter. And for you – for your silence."

THE ATTACK

"If he doesn't come today, I will have to decline your help, Balthazar, and engage people who are more deft and reliable," Zurita said, tugging impatiently at his mustache.

He was dressed in a white city suit and Panama hat. He met with Balthazar just outside of Buenos Aires, where the fields ended and pampas began.

Balthazar, dressed in a white shirt and blue striped pants, sat by the road quietly, picking at the sun-scorched grass.

He was beginning to regret sending his brother Christo to spy on Salvator.

Christo was ten years older than Balthazar. Despite his age, Christo was still strong and agile. He was as cunning as a pampas cat. Still, he was not entirely reliable. He tried farming, but found it boring. He then opened a small pub at the port, but became too fond of wine and soon went bankrupt.

In the last few years Christo engaged in various illegal dealings, using his superior cunning and sometimes treachery. Such a man was a suitable spy, but he could not be trusted. He was capable of betraying his own brother, if there was something in it for him. Balthazar knew it and was as concerned as Zurita.

"Are you sure Christo saw the balloon you released?"

Balthazar shrugged. He wanted to abandon this whole thing, go home, have some cold water with wine, and go to bed early.

The last rays of the setting sun lit up clouds of dust rising from beyond the hill. At the same time they heard a long shrill whistle.

Balthazar looked up, "It's him!"

"Finally!"

Christo was walking toward them briskly. He no longer looked like a worn out old Indian. Having whistled one more time, Christo said hello to Balthazar and Zurita.

"Well, have you met the Sea Devil?" Zurita asked him.

"Not yet, but he is there. Salvator keeps the Devil well hidden. But the main thing is done – I serve Salvator, and he trusts me. It didn't go so well with the sick granddaughter," Christo laughed. "She almost ruined the whole thing when she got better. I was hugging and kissing her like a loving grandpa, and this little fool started fighting and crying." Christo laughed again.

"Where did you get this granddaughter?" Zurita asked.

"The only thing hard to find is money. But there are plenty of little girls around," Christo replied. "The kid's mother is happy. I got five paper pesos from her, and she got a healthy daughter."

Christo neglected to mention receiving the heavy pouch of gold pesos from Salvator. Naturally, he had no intention of giving the money to the girl's mother.

"I've seen some strange things at Salvator's. A real zoo." Christo started telling them about everything he had seen.

"This is all very interesting," Zurita said, lighting a cigar, "but you haven't seen the main thing – the Devil. What are you planning to do next, Christo?"

"Next? We are going on a little trip to the Andes." And Christo told them that Salvator was planning to go get more animals.

"Excellent!" Zurita exclaimed. "Salvator's property is away from the settlements. In his absence, we will attack Salvator's house and kidnap the Sea Devil."

Christo shook his head, "The jaguars will rip your head off, and you won't be able to find the Devil. You won't even find him with your head still attached, because I haven't."

"Then here is a thought," Zurita said after a pause, "we can ambush him during the hunt and hold him prisoner until he gives us the Sea Devil."

Christo deftly pulled another cigar from Zurita's pocket.

"Thank you. An ambush is a better idea. But Salvator will deceive you – he will promise the ransom and won't pay up. Those Spaniards..." Christo coughed.

"Then what do you suggest?" Zurita asked irritably.

"Patience, Zurita. Salvator trusts me, but only to the fourth wall. The doctor must come to trust me as himself, and then he will show me the Devil."

"Well?"

"Salvator will be attacked by bandits," and Christo pointed at Zurita, "and I," he struck himself in the chest, "the honest Arauca, will save him. Then there will be no mysteries for Christo in Salvator's house." ("And my purse will be filled with golden pesos," he finished to himself.)

"Well, it's not a bad idea."

They agreed on the route Christo and Salvator would follow.

"The day before we leave, I will throw a red rock over the fence. Be prepared."

Despite the careful planning, one unforeseen circumstance almost ruined the entire undertaking.

Zurita, Balthazar, and ten thugs they hired at the port got dressed as Gaucho, armed themselves and waited for their victim on horseback.

It was dark. The riders listened, expecting to hear hoof beat. But Christo did not know that Salvator hunted differently from the way it was done several years ago.

The gang suddenly heard the sound of a swiftly approaching engine. Headlights flashed blindingly from beyond a hill. An enormous black car flew by the riders before they realized what happened.

Zurita cursed. Balthazar thought it funny.

"Don't be so upset, Pedro," the Indian said. "It's hot during the day, they are traveling at night with two suns in the front of Salvator's car. They will rest during the day. We can catch up to them at their campsite." Balthazar kicked his horse and rode after the car.

The others followed.

Two hours later, the riders suddenly noticed a fire in the distance.

"It's them. Something must have happened. Wait here, I shall crawl forward and find out. Wait for me."

Balthazar hopped off his horse and slithered forward like an eel. He returned in an hour.

"The car broke down. Something is wrong with it. They are fixing it. Christo is keeping watch. We must hurry."

Everything else happened very quickly. The thugs attacked. Before Salvator knew what was going on, he, Christo, and three of their companions were tied up.

One of the mercenaries, the leader of the gang demanded a large ransom from Salvator (Zurita preferred to hang back.)

"I will pay, let me go," Salvator replied.

"That's just for you. But you must pay as much for your friends!" the thug demanded.

"I cannot give you such a large sum all at once," Salvator replied after a pause.

"Kill him!" the rest of the gang shouted.

"If you don't accept our conditions, we'll kill you in the morning," the leader said.

Salvator shrugged and replied, "I don't have this much money with me."

Salvator's calm demeanor impressed even the gang leader.

Having left the captives behind the car, the thugs started looking around and found large quantities of alcohol for the samples. They drank the alcohol and collapsed.

Shortly before dawn, someone crawled carefully toward Salvator.

"It's me," Christo said quietly. "I managed to undo my straps. I got to the scoundrel with the gun and killed him. The rest are drunk. The driver fixed the car. We must hurry."

Everyone quickly got into the car, the driver revved up the engine, the car took off and sped up down the road.

They heard shouts and gun shots behind them.

Salvator shook Christo's hands.

Only after Salvator's departure Zurita found out from his mercenaries, that Salvator was willing to pay the ransom. *"It would have been easier,"* Zurita thought, *"to get the ransom rather than trying to kidnap the Sea Devil. We don't even know what he is."* But the opportunity was lost, and all he could do was wait for news from Christo.

Christo hoped that Salvator would walk up to him and say, "Christo, you saved my life. I have no secrets from you. Come, I'll show you the Sea Devil."

But Salvator had no intention of doing that. He generously rewarded Christo for the rescue, and then became absorbed in his scientific work.

Without wasting any time, Christo started studying the fourth wall and the secret door. He struggled for a long time, but finally Christo managed to solve the riddle. One time, as he was examining the door, he pressed on a small protrusion. The door suddenly gave way and opened. It turned out to be very thick and heavy like that of a safe. Christo quickly slipped through the opening, and the door instantly slammed shut behind him. This puzzled him. He looked over the door, pressed on various spots but the door refused to open.

"I trapped myself," Christo grumbled.

He had no other choice but to examine this last of Salvator's mysterious gardens.

Christo was in an overgrown area. The garden was in the shape of a basin surrounded by tall walls made of rocks. He could hear not only the surf but the rustling of pebbles across the sand.

The trees and shrubs growing here were typical for damp soil. Many creeks flowed among the sprawling trees providing plenty of shade. Dozens of fountains moistened the air. It was as humid as on the shores of Mississippi. In the middle of the garden stood a modest stone house with a flat roof. Its walls were covered with ivy. Green shutters covered the windows. The house looked to be deserted.

Christo reached the other side of the garden. By the wall separating the property from the bay there was a huge square pool surrounded by trees. It covered the area no less than five thousand square feet and was at least fifteen feet deep.

As Christo approached, some creature darted from the trees and dove into the pool, raising huge spray of water. Christo halted. It was him. The Sea Devil. Finally Christo would see him.

The Indian walked to the pool and looked through the transparent water.

At the bottom of the pool, on the white stone tiles, sat a large monkey. It gazed at Christo from underwater with alarm and curiosity. Christo was beside himself with astonishment – the monkey was breathing underwater. Its sides were rising and falling.

Having recovered from his initial surprise, Christo laughed – the Sea Devil that terrorized the fishermen turned out to be the amphibian monkey. *"The things that are possible in this world,"* the old Indian thought.

Christo was pleased – he finally managed to find out everything. But he was also disappointed. The monkey looked nothing like the monster described by the eyewitnesses. The things that fear and imagination could do!

He had to think of getting back. Christo returned to the door, climbed a tall tree by the wall and, at the risk of breaking his legs, jumped down on the other side.

As soon as he recovered his footing, he heard Salvator's voice," Christo! Where are you?"

Christo grabbed a rake he left by the path and started raking dry leaves.

"Here I am."

"Come, Christo," Salvator said, coming to the hidden metal door in the rock. "Look, this is how you open this door." Salvator pressed the spot Christo was already familiar with.

"The doctor is too late – I have already found the Devil," Christo thought.

Salvator and Christo entered the garden. They passed the house covered with ivy and headed to the pool. The monkey was still sitting in the water blowing bubbles.

Christo exclaimed in surprise, as if this was the first time he saw it. But what followed caused him to be even more astonished.

Salvator paid no attention to the monkey. He waved at it as if it was in his way. The monkey swam to the edge, climbed out of the pool, shook itself off, and climbed a nearby tree. Salvator leaned forward, ran his hand through the grass and pressed a small green tile. There was a dull noise. Holes opened in the bottom of the pool along the edges. In a few minutes, the pool was empty, and the openings slammed shut. A metal ladder leading to the bottom of the pool appeared from somewhere.

"Come, Christo."

40

They descended into the pool. Salvator stepped onto a tile, and another opening appeared in the middle of the pool, approximately ten square feet in size. Metal steps were leading underground.

Christo followed Salvator into this vault. They walked for quite some time. Weak scattered light fell through the hatch. But soon, even that light disappeared and they found themselves in complete darkness. Their footsteps echoed in the underground passageway.

"Watch your step, Christo, we are almost there."

Salvator stopped and ran his hand over the wall. A switch clicked, and bright light flared up. They were in a stalactite cave, in front of a door with door handles in the shape of lion heads holding metal rings in their teeth. Salvator pulled one of the rings. The heavy door opened smoothly and they entered a dark hall. Another switch clicked. A globe of frosted glass lit a vast cavern with one wall made entirely of glass. Salvator changed the light – the cavern grew dark while strong floodlights lit the space beyond the glass wall. This was an enormous aquarium, or rather, a glass house at the bottom of the ocean. Seaweed and coral rose from the sand with fish playing among them. Suddenly, Christo saw a human-like creature with large paws emerging from behind the coral growth. The stranger's body sparkled with bluish silver scales. Swiftly and deftly the creature swam to the glass wall, nodded to Salvator, and entered a glass chamber off to the side, closing the door. They heard water draining from the chamber. The stranger opened the second door and entered the grotto.

"Take off your glasses and gloves," Salvator said. The stranger obediently removed glasses and gloves, and Christo saw a handsome, slender young man.

"Meet Ichtiander, man-fish, or rather, the amphibian man, also known as the Sea Devil," Salvator introduced the young man.

The boy smiled, held out his hand to the Indian and said in Spanish, "Hello!"

Christo silently shook his hand. He was so shocked he couldn't speak.

"Ichtiander's regular servant is sick," Salvator continued. "I shall leave you with Ichtiander for a few days. If you manage your new duties well, I will assign you to Ichtiander permanently."

Christo nodded.

41

ICHTIANDER'S DAY

It was still dark, but dawn was coming.

The air was warm and humid, filled with the sweet scent of magnolias, tuberoses, and mignonettes. Not a single leaf moved. All was quiet. Ichtiander walked down one of the sandy garden paths. His dagger, glasses, and gloves that looked like frog hands swung from his belt. Crushed seashells crackled under his feet. The path was barely visible, surrounded by dark shapeless forms that were trees and shrubs. Fog floated above the pools. Sometimes Ichtiander brushed against a branch and it showered his hair and warm cheek with dew.

The path took a sharp turn and sloped down. The air turned cooler and wetter. Ichtiander felt stone tiles under his feet, slowed down, and finally stopped. He slowly put on his big glasses with thick lenses, gloves and flippers. He exhaled and jumped into the pool. Water wrapped him in pleasant coolness and prickled his gills. His gill slits started moving – the man turned into a fish.

With a few strong arm movements Ichtiander found himself at the bottom of the pool.

The young man confidently swam in complete darkness. He reached out and found a metal bracket in the stone wall, and another one next to it, then the third one. Following the brackets, he made it to a tunnel filled with water. He walked along the bottom to overcome a cold oncoming current. He then pushed away, floated up and reached what felt like warm bath water. The water heated in the garden pools flowed at the top of the tunnel toward the ocean. Now Ichtiander could swim with the current. He crossed his arms, rolled over onto his back, and floated along, head first.

The end of the tunnel was close. There, right next to the outlet to the ocean, a hot spring burst from a crack in the rock at high pressure. Small stones and shells rustled in its roiling stream.

Ichtiander rolled over onto his belly and looked forward. It was still dark. He reached out once again and felt the water grow cooler. His palm touched the metal grate, whose bars were covered with soft and slippery sea weed and coarse shells. Clutching the grate, the youth found the complex lock and opened it. The heavy round grate blocking the tunnel slowly opened. Ichtiander slipped through and the grate slammed shut.

The amphibian man headed toward the ocean, propelling himself with arms and legs. He was still surrounded by darkness, save for a few bluish pilot fish and dark red jellyfish. But morning was coming, and luminous creatures were putting out their lights one after another.

Ichtiander felt thousands of small prickles in his gills, and his breathing became more labored. This meant he was past the rocky cape. Beyond the cape, sea water was polluted with particles of clay, sand and various other things. The water was also less salty – they were close to a river delta.

"It's amazing how the river fish can live in the dirty fresh water," Ichtiander thought. "Their gills must not be as sensitive to the sand and silt."

Ichtiander rose higher, took a sharp turn to the right, to the south, then dove deeper. Water was cleaner here. Ichtiander found a cold underwater current flowing along the shore from south to north, until it reached the delta of the river Parana, which caused it to deviate to the east. This current flowed in deep waters, but its top boundary was only forty-five to sixty feet from the surface. Once again Ichtiander surrendered to the current and allowed it to carry him far into the ocean.

He could take a short nap. There was no danger – it was still dark, and the predators were still asleep. It was nice to doze off before sunrise. His skin could sense the changes in water temperature and underwater currents.

His ear caught a dull rumbling sound, and another one, and another one. These were anchor chains – fishing boats were setting sail in the bay a few miles away. Dawn was near. And there was the measured distant thunder. These were the propeller and the engines of *Gorrox* – a large English ocean liner traveling between Buenos Aires and Liverpool. *Gorrox* was still twenty-five miles away. But he could hear it clearly! Sound traveled through sea water at almost five thousand feet per second. At night *Gorrox* was particularly beautiful – a real floating city filled with dazzling lights! But in order to see it at night, he would have to go out far into the ocean the evening before. *Gorrox* arrived to Buenos Aires in the morning, its lights already out. No, there was no more napping – *Gorrox*'s propellers, steering rods, and engines, the vibrations of its hull, and the lights from the portholes were bound to wake up other ocean dwellers. The dolphins had to be the first to hear the approaching

Gorrox and caused a few strong ripples with their jumping, alerting Ichtiander. They had to be on their way to the ship.

The drumbeat of various motors could now be heard from various directions – the port and the bay were waking up. Ichtiander opened his eyes, shook his head as if to get rid of the last of his drowsiness, swung his arms, pushed with his legs and rose to the surface.

He carefully looked out of the water and glanced around. There were neither boats nor schooners nearby. He emerged up to his waist and bobbed in the water, slowly moving his legs.

Gannets and seagulls flew low above the water, sometimes brushing against its surface with their chest or one wing and leaving behind slowly rolling circles. The white seagulls sounded like crying children. An enormous snow-white albatross flew over Ichtiander's head, its huge wings whistling and creating a breeze in its wake. Its primary feathers were tipped with black, its beak was red and yellow, and its feet were orange. It headed toward the bay. Ichtiander gazed after it with some jealousy. The bird's black-edged wings had a span of at least twelve feet. He wished he could have wings like that!

In the west, night was rolling beyond the distant mountains. The east was turning crimson. Barely noticeable, calm ripples appeared on the surface of the ocean, with veins of gold in between. White seagulls rose higher and turned pink. Colorful streams in various shades of blue snaked over the pale smoothness of water under the first gusts of wind. There were more and more of them. The wind grew stronger. Yellow-white tongues of surf appeared on the sandy shore, and the water turned green.

An entire fleet of fishing boats approached. His father ordered him to avoid being seen. Ichtiander dove and once again found the cold current. It carried him farther away from the shore, to the east, into the open ocean. All around him was the bluish-purple deep ocean darkness. The fish around him looked pale-green, with dark spots and stripes. More fish – red, yellow, gold, and brown – darted around him like colorful butterflies.

He heard a rumbling from above, and saw a dark shadow on the water. It was a military hydroplane flying low above the ocean.

One time, one such hydroplane landed on the water. Ichtiander grabbed one of the metal floats and nearly paid with his life when the hydroplane suddenly took off. Ichtiander had to jump from a height of thirty feet.

Ichtiander looked up. He could see the sun almost directly above his head. It was almost noon. The water surface no longer resembled a smooth mirror reflecting every stone, large fish, and Ichtiander himself. Now, the mirror was twisting, flexing, and constantly moving.

Ichtiander floated up. The waves rocked him. He peeked out from the water, rose on the crest of a wave, slid down, rose again. Look at that! The surf by the beach was rustling, roaring, and rolling large stones. The water turned yellow-green. A brisk south-western wind was blowing. The waves were getting bigger, tipped with white foam. Ichtiander was showered with splashes of water and enjoyed it.

"Why is it," Ichtiander thought, "that when you swim at the waves, they look dark-blue, but when you look back at them, they are much paler?"

A school of fish took off from a wave crest – these were long-finned flying fish. Rising and falling, by passing the tops of the waves and the gaps between them, the flyers traveled at least three hundred feet, then dropped into the water only to emerge in a minute or two. The white seagulls kept darting around and weeping. The swiftest of all birds – the frigate birds – sliced through the air with their wide wings. One of them had a huge hooked beak, sharp talons, dark-brown feathers tinged with metallic green, and an orange chest. That was the male. Not far from him was another frigate bird – paler, with a white chest – the female. Suddenly, she dropped into the water like a rock, and emerged in a second with a silver-blue fish thrashing in its hooked beak. The albatrosses were also nearby foretelling a storm. High above a wonderful brave bird – the Southern screamer – was rushing toward the storm cloud. It always greeted the storm with its song. But fishing boats and the pretty yacht rushed toward the shore to hide from the storm.

All was greenish twilight under the way, but he could still see the sun through the thickness of water as a large pale spot. This was enough to figure out his direction. He had to make it to the sand bar before the cloud covered the sun, otherwise there would be no breakfast for him. It's been a while since he had eaten, and he could not find the sand bar or the underwater rocks in the dark. Ichtiander's arms and legs were working hard – he was swimming like a frog.

From time to time, he rolled over onto his back and checked his direction by the barely noticeably streak of light in the thick blue-green darkness. Sometimes he peered ahead to check for the sand bar. His gills and his skin could sense a change in the water – by the sand bar, it was lighter, less salty, and more saturated with oxygen. Pleasant-feeling, light water. He tasted the water. At that moment, he was much like an old experienced sailor, who could tell that he wasn't far from land even when he couldn't see it, using his own signs and markers.

Gradually, the water around him grew brighter. To the right and to the left loomed the familiar outlines of the underground rocks. Between them was a small plateau with a rock wall behind it. Ichtiander called this spot his underwater harbor. It remained quiet even in the worst storms.

The quiet underwater harbor was crowded with fish! They swarmed as if in a roiling pot of fish soup. Small ones, dark, with a yellow stripe across their bodies and yellow tails, others with slanting dark stripes, red, blue, purple. They vanished suddenly, then reappeared just as unexpectedly in the same spot. When he floated up and looked around, he was surrounded by fish, but when he looked down, the fish were gone without a trace. It took Ichtiander a long time to understand how this happened, until one time he caught one of these fish. Its body was the size of his hand, but completely flat. This was why the fish were hard to see from above.

There was breakfast – the smooth plateau by the rocky wall was covered with oysters. Ichtiander swam closer, stretched out next to the shells and started eating. He pulled the oysters from their shells and swallowed them whole. He was used to eating underwater by placing something into his mouth, then deftly pushing the water out through half-closed lips. He did swallow a little bit of water with his food, but he was used to it.

All around him floated the seaweed – the hole-riddled green agar leaves, the feathery green algae, the delicate pink anemones. Presently, they all looked dark-grey – the water was nothing but twilight from the continuing thunderstorm. From time to time he could hear thunder. Ichtiander looked up.

Why was it so dark suddenly? A dark spot appeared right above Ichtiander's head. What could it be? He was finished with his breakfast and could now take a look at the surface. Ichtiander carefully floated up to the dark spot above him, gliding along the sheer rock wall. It turned out that an enormous albatross settled onto the water surface. The bird's orange feet were very close to Ichtiander. He reached up and grabbed the albatross' feet. The frightened bird opened its powerful wings and rose, pulling Ichtiander out of the water. But Ichtiander's body turned instantly heavy in the air, and the albatross fell back into the water, covering him with its soft feathery body. Ichtiander decided not to wait for the albatross to peck him in the head with its red beak, dove, and surfaced again in another spot. The albatross flew off to the east and vanished behind the water mountains raised by the raging storm.

Ichtiander rested on his back. The thunderstorm had passed. The thunder was rumbling somewhere far in the east. But it was still pouring rain. Ichtiander squinted with pleasure. He finally opened his eyes, turned to stand in the water and looked around. He was at the crest of a tall wave. The sky, the ocean, the wind, the clouds, the rain, the waves – everything around him merged into a wet rolling bundle that was humming, rustling, roaring, and rumbling. The foam curled at the wave crests and snaked angrily between them. Water peaks rushed swiftly forward and crashed down like avalanches, more waves rose, rain fell, wind howled desperately.

What would frighten an ordinary person was a joy to Ichtiander. Of course, he had to be careful, otherwise he could be crushed by a wave. But Ichtiander knew how to deal with the waves as well as any fish. He just had to recognize them – one carried him up and down, another one tried to flip him over. He also knew how to swim under the waves and how the waves went away when the storm was over – first the small ones, then the large ones, but the measured slow ripples stayed around for a long time. He loved to tumble in the surf, but knew that it was dangerous. One time, a wave suddenly flipped Ichtiander over, he hit his head and fainted. Another person would have drowned, but Ichtiander recovered underwater.

The rain stopped. It was carried off to the east along with the storm. The wind changed. Warm air flew in from the tropical north. Pieces of blue sky appeared between the clouds. Sunlight broke through and hit the waves. A double rainbow appeared in the still-dark and gloomy south-eastern sky. The ocean was transformed. It was no longer lead-colored, but dark-blue with bright-green spots in the places lit by the sun.

Sunlight! In one moment it transformed the sky and the ocean, the shore and the distant mountains. The air was so wonderful, light, and

47

moist after the storm! Ichtiander kept switching between the clean, healthy sea air and breathing with his gills. Ichtiander was the only one of all people who knew how easy it was to breathe after the storm, the rain, the wind, and the waves mixed the sky and the ocean, the air and the water, and saturated the water with oxygen. Everything came alive then – all the fish and all the other underwater creatures.

After the storm, small fish appeared from the narrow cracks and from the thickets of fanciful corals and sea sponges, followed by the larger fish, and finally, when all was completely calm and quiet, by the fragile, delicate jellyfish, transparent, almost weightless crawfish, siphonophores, ctenophores, and Venus ribbons.

A sunbeam fell onto a wave. Water around it turned instantly green, small bubbles sparkled, foam hissed. Not far from Ichtiander his friends the dolphins were playing, glancing at him with their merry, mischievous, and curious eyes. Their dark glossy backs popped up here and there among the waves. They splashed, snorted, and chased each other. Ichtiander laughed and went to chase the dolphins, swimming and diving along with them. He felt as if the ocean, the dolphins, the sky, and the sun were made just for him

***

Ichtiander looked up at the sun and squinted. It was traveling toward the west. Soon it would be evening. But he did not wish to go home early. He wanted to float just like that, until the sky grew dark and the stars appeared.

But soon he became bored from inaction. Not far from him, small sea creatures were dying. He could save them. He rolled over and looked at the distant shore. There, by the sand bar! His assistance was needed there, where the surf was the harshest.

This crazy surf threw piles of seaweed and sea dwellers onto the shore after every storm – jellyfish, crabs, starfish, and an occasional careless dolphin. The jellyfish died very quickly, some fish managed to make it to the water, but many perished on the shore. The crabs almost always returned into the ocean. Sometimes they came out on purpose to hunt the victims of the surf. Ichtiander liked saving the beached sea animals.

For hours he walked up and down the beach and rescued those who could still be saved. He was glad when a fish he threw in the water swam away with a merry flip of a tail. He was happy every time when the half-dead fish floating sideways or belly up finally came back to life. When he found a large fish, Ichtiander picked it up with both hands and carried it to the water. The fish thrashed in his hands, and he laughed and tried convincing it to be still and wait a little longer. Of course, he would have happily eaten this very same fish, had he caught it in the ocean. But that would have been necessary evil. Here, on the shore, he was the benefactor, the friend, and the savior of the sea dwellers.

Usually, Ichtiander returned the same way he left – using the underwater current. But today, he didn't want to go underwater – the ocean and the sky were too beautiful. The youth dove, swam underwater, then resurfaced, like sea birds hunting fish.

The last rays of sun faded. A strip of yellow burned in the west for a long time. Gloomy waves followed one after another, like dark-gray shadows.

Compared to the cool air, water was very warm. It was dark, but not scary. No one would attack him at this hour. The diurnal predators were already asleep, and the nocturnal ones hadn't come out to hunt yet.

Here was what he wanted – the northern current very close to the surface of the ocean. The steady post-storm ripples rocked this underwater river up and down, but it still flowed slowly from the hot north to the cold south. Far below was a reverse current – from south to north. Ichtiander used these currents often when he had to swim along the shore for a long time.

Today, he ended up far to the north from home. Now, this warm current would take him all the way to the tunnel. He just had to stay awake and make sure he didn't miss the entrance, which had happened to him in the past. He folded his arms behind his head, then stretched them to the sides, opened and closed his legs for exercise. The current carried him south. The warm water and the slow movements of his arms and legs had a soothing effect.

Ichtiander looked up – the water surface before him was scattered with stars, as small as dust. These were pilot fish turning on their luminaries and rising to the surface of the ocean. Here and there in the darkness were glowing blue and pink nebulae – dense clusters of tiny luminous creatures. Globes of soft green light slowly floated by. Very close to Ichtiander bobbed a jellyfish – it looked like a lamp with a fanciful shade, tipped with lace and a long fringe. The fringe rocked slowly with the jellyfish's every movement, as if in a light wind. Starfish shone brightly at the sand bars. Lights were moving down in the deep – those belonged to large nocturnal predators. They were chasing each other, twirling, fading, then flaring up again.

Another sand bar. Fanciful coral trunks and branches were lit from within with blue, pink, green, and white lights. Some corals shone with pale flickering glow, others were like white hot metal.

Nights on earth had only the small distant stars and sometimes the moon. But here, there were thousands of stars, thousands of the moons, thousands of tiny colorful suns, glowing with soft, delicate light. The underwater nights were incomparably more beautiful than those ashore.

Ichtiander floated to the surface to compare the two.

The air grew warmer. Above him was the dark-blue sky scattered with stars. Above the horizon hung the silver moon, casting a band of light across the ocean.

A long, low and deep horn sounded from the port. The giant *Gorrox* was getting ready for its return voyage. It was very late! Almost down. Ichtiander was absent almost an entire day. His father was bound to scold him.

Ichtiander headed toward the tunnel, put his hand between the bars, opened the metal grate and swam through the tunnel in complete darkness. When returning, he had to use the deeper, cold current from the sea to the garden pools.

A light nudge on the shoulder woke him up. He was in the pool. He swiftly floated up and switched to breathing with his lungs, inhaling the air filled with familiar flower scents.

In a few minutes he was asleep in his bed, as his father ordered.

A GIRL AND A DARK MAN

One time, he was swimming in the ocean after a thunderstorm.

When he surfaced, Ichtiander noticed an object in the waves not far away from him that looked like a piece of sail torn by the storm from a fishing schooner. Having gotten closer he realized with surprise that it was a human being – a young woman. She was tied to a plank.

Was this beautiful girl dead? Ichtiander was so agitated by this find that for the first time he felt animosity toward the ocean.

Perhaps, the girl was just unconscious. He adjusted her helplessly hanging head, grabbed the plank and swam to the shore.

He went as fast as he could, straining to the limit, only pausing briefly to adjust the girl's head as it inched off the plank.

He whispered to her, as he would to a beached fish, "Just wait a little longer!" He wanted for the girl to open her eyes, but he was also afraid of it. He wanted to make certain she was alive, but didn't want to scare her. Should he take off his glasses and gloves? But that would take time, and it would be harder to swim without the gloves. He resumed his swimming, pushing the plank with the girl toward the shore.

Finally he reached the surf line. He knew he had to be careful. The waves carried him to the shore. From time to time Ichtiander stretched out one leg to feel for the bottom. Finally, he reached shallow water, carried the girl to the shore, untied her from the plank, carried her into the shade of a brush-covered dune and started reviving her with CPR.

He thought he saw her eyelids tremble and her eyelashes move. Ichtiander pressed his ear to the girl's chest and heard a weak beating. She was alive. He wanted to scream with joy.

The girl opened her eyes, looked at Ichtiander, and an expression of horror appeared on her face. Then her eyes closed again. Ichtiander was both happy and sad. He saved her after all. But now he had to leave to keep from scaring her. How could he leave her alone, so helpless? While he thought about it, he heard someone's swift heavy footsteps. He could delay no longer.

Ichtiander dove into the surf, swam underwater toward a line of rocks, surfaced and watched the shore while hiding between the rocks.

A dark swarthy man with mustache and a goatee, with a wide-brimmed hat on his head walked out from behind the dune. He said quietly in Spanish, "Here she is, praise Jesus!" He almost ran to her, then suddenly took a sharp turn to the ocean and walked into the surf. Soaking wet, he ran back to the girl and started doing CPR (whatever for?). He leaned toward her and kissed her. Then he started speaking quickly and heatedly. Ichtiander could hear only a few words, "I warned you... It was madness... At least I knew to tie you to the plank..."

The girl opened her eyes and raised her head. On her face, fear was replaced by surprised, then anger, then displeasure. The man with the goatee kept talking and helped the girl to her feet. But she was still too weak and he let her sit down on the sand. In half an hour they finally set out. They passed near the rocks where Ichtiander was hiding. The girl frowned and said to the man in the big hat, "Then it was you who saved me? Thank you. May God smile upon you!"

"I wish you, and not God, would smile upon me," the dark man said.

The girl seemed not to hear these words. She paused and then said, "Strange. I thought... I imagined that there was some sort of monster next to me."

"Of course you imagined it," her companion replied. "Or, perhaps, it was the Sea Devil who thought you were dead and tried to steal your soul. Say a prayer and lean on me. Not a single devil will dare touch you, while you are with me."

They walked away – the wonderful girl and that wicked dark man who convinced her that he saved her. But Ichtiander could not confront him. They were free to do as they wished – Ichtiander's job was done.

The girl and her companion disappeared behind the dunes, and Ichtiander was still gazing after them. He then turned toward the ocean. It seemed so big and deserted!

The surf tossed a blue fish with a silver belly onto the sand. Ichtiander glanced around – he was alone. He ran out of his hiding place, grabbed the fish and threw it back into the ocean. The fish swam away, but Ichtiander felt sad for some reason. He wandered around the deserted shore, picked up fish and starfish and carried them to the water. Gradually, he became absorbed with his work. His usual good mood was returning. He worked until evening, returning into the water only when the shore wind started burning and drying his gills.

ICHTIANDER'S SERVANT

Salvator decided to go to the mountains without Christo, who was doing well serving Ichtiander. The Indian was very glad – in Salvator's absence he would have an easier time meeting with Balthazar. Christo had already informed Balthazar that he found the Sea Devil. They just had to figure out how to kidnap Ichtiander.

Christo now lived in the white ivy-covered cottage and saw Ichtiander often. They quickly became friends. Ichtiander, deprived of company, became attached to the old Indian, who told him much about life on solid ground. Ichtiander knew more about the sea than the most famous scientists, and he told Christo the secrets of the underwater world. Ichtiander was fairly well-versed in geography, he knew oceans, seas, and the largest rivers; he also had some knowledge of astronomy, navigation, physics, botany, and zoology. But he knew very little about people – a little bit about the races inhabiting the Earth, with a vague notion about history and a five-year old child's understanding of political and economic relations. During the day, when it grew hot, Ichtiander went into the underground grotto and swam away. He returned to the white cottage only when the heat subsided and remained there until morning. If it rained or if the seas were stormy, he often spent an entire day at the cottage. He felt well enough outside of water when the weather was wet.

The cottage was not very big, with only four rooms. Christo occupied the room by the kitchen. Next to it was a dining room, followed by a large library – Ichtiander spoke Spanish and English. The last and the largest room was Ichtiander's bedroom. In the middle of the bedroom was a pool. There was a bed next to the wall. Sometimes Ichtiander slept in bed, but he preferred the pool. However, before Salvator left, he ordered Christo to make certain that Ichtiander slept in bed at least three nights a week. In the evening, Christo came to see Ichtiander and grumbled like an old nanny, when the boy refused to sleep in bed.

"But it's so much nicer and more comfortable sleeping in the water," Ichtiander protested.

"The doctor said that you should sleep in bed – you must listen to your father."

Ichtiander called Salvator his father, but Christo questioned their relationship. The skin on Ichtiander's face was fairly pale, but, perhaps, it went pale from prolonged exposure to water. Ichtiander's regular features, straight nose, thin lips, and large bright eyes resembled that of an Arauca – the tribe Christo himself was a member of.

Christo wished he could check the color of the rest of Ichtiander's skin, but it was covered by the scale-like suit made out of some unknown material.

"Why don't you take off your scales overnight?" he asked the boy.

"What for? My scales cause me no trouble, the suit is very comfortable. It doesn't prevent my gills and skin from breathing, but is also a good protection – it can't be cut either by a shark's tooth or by a knife," Ichtiander replied, getting into bed.

"Why do you wear the glasses and the gloves?" Christo asked, examining the webbed gloves on the nightstand.

They were made of greenish rubber, the fingers were extended using jointed sticks coated in rubber, and connected with webbing. The flippers for the feet were even longer.

"The gloves help me swim faster. And the glasses protect my eyes when a storm stirs up the sand from the ocean floor. I don't always wear them. But I do see better underwater with the glasses on. Without them, everything looks foggy."

Ichtiander smiled and continued, "When I was little, father sometimes allowed me to play with the children living in the next garden. I was very surprised when I saw them swimming in the pool without the gloves. 'How can you swim like that?' I asked them. But they couldn't understand what gloves I was talking about, because I didn't swim in front of them."

"Do you still go out into the bay?" Christo asked.

"Of course. I just use a side underwater tunnel. Some mean people almost caught me with their nets, and now I have to be very careful."

"Hm… Then there is another tunnel leading into the bay?"

"Several of them. It's too bad you can't swim with me! I could show you some amazing things. Why can't all people live underwater? We could take a ride on my ocean horse."

"Your ocean horse? What is that?"

"My dolphin. I tamed him. Poor fellow! He was beached by a storm once, and his fin was badly bruised. I dragged him into the water. It was hard – dolphins are so much heavier on dry land than they are in the water. Everything here is heavier. Even my own body. It's easier in the water. Anyway, I dragged the dolphin back into the ocean, but he couldn't swim, which meant he couldn't feed himself. I fed him fish for a long time, a whole month. In that time, he not only got used to me, but became attached to me. We became friends. Other dolphins know me too. It's so much fun playing around in the ocean with the dolphins! Waves, spray, sunlight, wind, noise! It's nice at the ocean floor too. It's as if you are flying through thick blue air. It's quiet. You can't feel your own body. It becomes free, light, capable of the slightest movement. I have many friends at sea. I feed small fish like you feed birds – they follow me everywhere."

"What about enemies?"

"I have enemies too. Sharks and octopi. But I am not afraid of them. I have my knife."

"What if they sneak up on you?"

Ichtiander was puzzled by this question.

"But I can hear them from the distance?"

"You can hear underwater?" it was Christo's turn to be puzzled. "Even when they swim very quietly?"

"Yes. What's so hard about that? I can hear with my ears and with my entire body. They make water vibrate, and these vibrations travel ahead of them. I feel the vibrations and turn to look."

"Even when you are asleep?"

"Of course."

"But the fish…"

"The fish die not from a sudden attack, but because they cannot escape or defend against a much stronger enemy. But I am stronger than all of them. And the sea predators know this. They don't dare come close to me."

"Zurita is right – this seagoing fellow is worth working for," Christo thought. "But it won't be easy catching him in the water. 'I can hear with my entire body!' He might get stuck in a trap, but unlikely. I should warn Zurita."

"Underwater world is very beautiful!" Ichtiander kept telling. "No, I shall never trade the sea for your stuffy, dusty land!"

"Why our land? You too were born on land," Christo said. "Who was your mother?"

"I don't know…" Ichtiander said hesitantly. "Father said she died when I was born."

"But she was a woman, of course, not a fish."

"Perhaps," Ichtiander agreed. Christo laughed.

"Now tell me, why did you cause mischief, scared the fishermen, cut their nets, and throw the fish out of the boats?"

"Because they caught more fish than they could eat."

"But they were fishing for sale." Ichtiander didn't understand.

"So that other people could eat too," the Indian explained.

"Are there really so many people?" Ichtiander wondered. "Don't they have enough birds and animals on the ground? Why do they come to the ocean?"

"I can't explain it right away," Christo said with a yawn. "It's time for bed. Make sure you don't climb into your tub, or your father will be mad." Christo left.

Early in the morning Christo discovered that Ichtiander was gone. The stone floor was wet.

"He slept in the pool again," the Indian grumbled. "And then probably went to the ocean."

Ichtiander was very late for breakfast. He was upset about something. Having picked at his steak with a fork he said, "Fried meat again."

"Yes, again," Christo replied sternly. "The doctor said so. Did you eat raw fish again? At this rate, you'll forget how to eat cooked food. And you slept in your tub again. If you don't sleep in bed, your gills will get out of habit of being in the air, and then you'll complain that your sides are prickling. And you were late for breakfast. When the doctor comes back, I'll tell him all about it. You have gotten completely out of hand."

"Don't tell him, Christo. I don't want to upset him." Ichtiander looked down and thought about something. When he looked back up, his large eyes were sad, as he said, "Christo, I saw a girl. I have never seen anything so beautiful – not even at the bottom of the ocean."

"Then why did you berate the land?" Christo said.

"I was riding my dolphin by the shore and saw her not far from Buenos Aires. She had blue eyes and golden hair." Ichtiander added after a pause, "She saw me, got scared and ran away. Why did I have to put on the glasses and the gloves?" He paused again, then said very quietly, "One time, I saved a girl who almost drowned in the ocean. I didn't notice what she looked like then. What if it was the same girl? I think she had golden hair too. Yes, yes... I remember..." The boy became pensive again, then walked to the mirror and looked at himself carefully for the first time.

"What did you do then?"

"I waited for her, but she didn't come back. Christo, will she never come back to the beach?"

"It's not a bad thing that he likes a girl," Christo thought. Until then, as much as Christo tried to talk up the city, he could not convince Ichtiander to go visit Buenos Aires, where Zurita could easily catch the boy.

"The girl might not come back, but I could help you find her. You can put on a suit and come to the city with me."

"Will I see her?" Ichtiander exclaimed.

"There are many girls there. Maybe you'll see the one from the beach."

"Let's go now!"

"It's late. It takes a long time to walk to the city."

"I can ride the dolphin, and you can follow along the shore."

"You are too hasty," Christo replied. "We shall set out together tomorrow, at dawn. You will swim out into the bay, and I'll await you on the shore with the suit. I still have to find a suit for you." (*"I'll have time to see my brother overnight,"* Christo thought.) "Tomorrow then. At dawn."

IN THE CITY

Ichtiander came out of the bay and onto the beach. Christo was already waiting for him with a white suit in his hands. Ichtiander looked at the suit as if someone was offering him to put on snake skin, sighed, and started getting dressed. Clearly, he didn't have to wear a suit very often. The Indian helped him tie his tie, looked Ichtiander over, and remained satisfied.

"Come," Christo said merrily.

The Indian wanted to impress Ichtiander and took him along the city's major streets – Avenida Alvar and Bertis. He showed him the Victoria Square with its cathedral and city hall built in the Mauritanian style, the Fuerto Square and May Twenty-Fifth Square with the Freedom Obelisque, the Presidential palace surrounded by beautiful trees.

But Christo was wrong. The noise, the city traffic, the dust, the heat, and the bustle completely overwhelmed Ichtiander. He tried to find the girl in the crowd, often grabbed Christo's hand and whispered, "It's her!" but then realized his mistake. "No, it's another girl."

It was noon. The heat was becoming intolerable. Christo suggested stopping by a small basement restaurant and having breakfast. It was cooler, but noisy and stuffy. Dirty, poorly dressed people were smoking vile-smelling cigars. Ichtiander was suffocating from the smoke, while everyone around them argued loudly, shaking newspapers and shouting strange words. Ichtiander drank a lot of cold water but didn't touch his breakfast and said sadly, "It's easier to find a fish in the ocean than a person in this human whirlpool. Your cities are revolting! They are stuffy and smell bad. My sides are hurting. I want to go home, Christo."

"Fine," Christo agreed. "Let's just stop to see a friend of mine and then we'll go back."

"I don't want to see anyone."

"It's along the way. I won't take long."

Having paid, Christo and Ichtiander walked out into the street. Looking down and breathing heavily, Ichtiander followed Christo past white buildings, past gardens with cacti, olives, and peach trees. The Indian was taking him to his brother Balthazar who lived at the new port.

As they came closer to the sea, Ichtiander inhaled the damp air. He wanted to pull off his clothes and dive into the water.

"We are almost there," Christo said, casting a concerned glance at his companion.

They crossed the railroad tracks.

"Here we are," Christo said, and they descended into a dark little shop.

When Ichtiander's eyes became accustomed to the twilight, he looked around in astonishment. The shop looked like a corner of the ocean floor. The shelves and even some of the floor were covered with shells – large and small, spiral and folding. Strings of coral hung from the ceiling, along with starfish, taxidermied fish, dried crabs, and other strange sea dwellers. On the counter under glass were pearls in boxes. One of the boxes held pink pearls – "angel's skin" as they were called by the divers. Ichtiander felt somewhat calmer among familiar things.

"Rest, it's cool and quiet here," Christo said, offering the boy an old wicker chair.

"Balthazar! Gutierre!" the Indian shouted.

"Is that you, Christo?" a voice responded from another room. "Come here."

Christo leaned down to enter a low door leading into the next room.

This was Balthazar's laboratory. Here he restored the color of pearls faded from the dampness by using a weak acid solution. Christo shut the door firmly behind him. Weak light fell through a small window by the ceiling, shedding light on vials and glass tubs on the old, blackened table.

"Hello, brother. Where is Gutierre?"

"She went to the neighbor to get an iron. Nothing but lace and bows on her mind. She'll be back shortly," Balthazar replied.

"And Zurita?" Christo asked impatiently.

"He went off somewhere, damn him. We had a little row yesterday."

"Because of Gutierre?"

"Zurita kept trying to reason with her. And she said the same thing, 'No, I don't want to!' What am I going to do with her? She is picky and stubborn. She thinks too much of herself. She doesn't understand that any tribal girl, even if she was the first beauty in town, would have been happy to marry a man like that. He has his own schooner, and a team of divers," Balthazar grumbled, bathing the pearls in the solution. "Zurita is probably drinking again, from sheer spite."

"What are we going to do?"

"Did you bring him?"

"He is here."

Balthazar came to the door and peeked through the keyhole.

"I can't see him," he said quietly.

"He is on a chair, by the counter."

"I can't see him. Gutierre is there."

Balthazar quickly opened the door and entered the shop with Christo. Ichtiander was gone. The girl, Balthazar's adopted daughter stood in the dark corner. Gutierre was known for her beauty far beyond the port neighborhood. But she was shy and willful. More often than not she said in a melodious but firm voice, "No!"

Pedro Zurita liked Gutierre. He wanted to marry her. And the old Balthazar didn't mind becoming family with someone who owned his own boat and possibly being appointed a partner. But to all of Zurita's proposals the girl invariably answered, "No." When her father and Christo entered the room, the girl was standing with her eyes downcast.

"Hello, Gutierre," Christo said.

"Where is the young man?" Balthazar asked.

"I don't hide young men," she replied with a smile. "When I came in, he looked at me very strangely, as if frightened, then rose, suddenly grabbed his chest, and ran away. Before I could say anything, he was out of the door."

"It was her," Christo thought.

BACK TO THE SEA

Ichtiander ran along the beach gasping for breath. Having broken free of this terrible city, he took a sharp turn and headed to the shore. He hid between the rocks, looked around, quickly undressed, hid the suit under the stones, ran to the water, and dove in.

Despite his fatigue, he never swam as fast as he did this time. The fish darted away from him in terror. Only when he was several miles from the city, Ichtiander rose closer to the surface and swam along the shore. He was more at home in this area. He knew every underwater rock and every crack in the ocean floor. There, sprawled on the sand lived the timid flounders, and over there were the red coral thickets hiding small red-finned fish in its branches. This sunken fishing boat became home to two squid families, and they recently had their young. Crabs hid under that pile of gray rocks. Ichtiander could spend hours watching them. He knew their small joys of successful hunt and their troubles, like a loss of a pincer or an attack by an octopus. There were many oyster shells by the shoreline rocks.

Finally, not far from the bay, Ichtiander stuck his head above water. He saw a school of dolphins playing in the waves and gave a long loud shout. A large dolphin snorted merrily in response and swiftly headed toward his friend, diving and resurfacing, his black glossy back flickering among the waves.

"Faster, Leading, faster!" Ichtiander shouted, swimming to meet him. "Let's go far away, come on!"

Obeying the man's pull, the dolphin swiftly headed into the open ocean, toward the wind and the waves. He sliced through the waves swiftly, but Ichtiander felt it wasn't enough.

"Come on, Leading! Faster, faster!"

Ichtiander drove the dolphin to exhaustion, but this mad ride across the way did not comfort him. He left his friend completely befuddled, having slipped off his glossy back and submerged into the ocean. The dolphin waited, snorted, dove, surfaced, snorted disdainfully once again, then took a sharp turn and headed toward the shore, glancing back from time to time. His friend never resurfaced, and Leading rejoined his school, greeted happily by young dolphins. Ichtiander went deeper and deeper into the twilight of the ocean. He wanted to be alone, recover from the new impressions, and sort out everything he had found out and seen. He ended up very far from home but didn't think about the danger. He wanted to understand why he wasn't like everyone else – a stranger to the ocean and to the land.

He submerged slower and slower. The water was becoming denser, it was beginning to press on him, and making it difficult to breathe. He was surrounded by thick, green-gray twilight. There were fewer sea dwellers here, and many were strangers to Ichtiander – he has never been this deep. For the first time Ichtiander felt spooky in this silent twilight world. He swiftly rose to the surface and headed toward the shore. The sun was setting, piercing the water with its red beams. In the water, these beams mixed with water and shimmered with delicate purple-pink and green-blue tones.

Ichtiander didn't have his glasses and saw the ocean surface the way the fish did – from underwater it appeared not flat, but cone-shaped, as if he was at the bottom of a huge funnel. The edges of this funnel seemed colored with red, yellow, green, blue and purple bands. Beyond the funnel was the smooth water surface, reflecting underwater objects like a mirror – rocks, seaweed, and fish.

Ichtiander rolled over onto his chest, swam to the shore, and settled down underwater between the rocks, not far from the sand bar. A group of fishermen stepped into the water and were pulling their boat onto the shore. One of them was up to his knees in water. Ichtiander could see what looked to be the legless fisherman above water, and his legs – separately underwater, as well as their reflection in the water surface. Another fisherman was in the water up to his shoulders. He looked like a strange, headless, four-legged creature, as if two identical people were beheaded and then placed onto each other's shoulders. When people walked to the shore, Ichtiander saw them the way the fish did – seemingly reflected in a globe. He could see them from head to foot before they reached the shore. ...Which was why he always managed to get away before people managed to notice him.

These strange bodies with four arms and no heads and heads with no bodies now seemed repulsive to Ichtiander. People... They were so noisy, they smoked terrible cigars, and smelled bad. No, the dolphins were better – they were clean and happy. Ichtiander smiled recalling the time he drank some dolphin milk.

There was a small bay far in the south. Sharp underwater rocks and a sand bar made it unsuitable for ships. The shore was rocky and steep there. This bay was never fished either by the fishermen or by the pearl divers. Its shallow bottom was covered with a thick carpet of seaweed. There was a lot of fish in its warm waters. A female dolphin came there several years in a row to give birth to her young in this warm bay – two, four, sometimes even six of them in a litter. Ichtiander was very amused by the young dolphins and he watched them for hours, hiding in the seaweed. The baby dolphins either tumbled on the surface or suckled their mother, pushing and shoving at each other with their snouts. Ichtiander started gradually taming them by catching small fish and feeding it to the young dolphins. Gradually, they and their mother became used to Ichtiander. He was able to play with the little ones, catch them, throw them, tumble them. They clearly enjoyed this – they followed him everywhere and dashed to him whenever they spotted him in the bay with handfuls of treats: small tasty fish and even tastier delicate young octopi.

Once, when the female had another litter and they were still very small – too small to eat anything and subsisting only with their mother's milk – Ichtiander thought why couldn't he try some dolphin milk.

He crept under the female, wrapped his arms around her and suckled. The dolphin didn't expect this and pulled away, terrified. Ichtiander instantly released the frightened animal. The milk had a strong fishy aftertaste. The frightened female, having freed herself from the uninvited suckling, dove deeper, and her babies became confused and darted this way and that. Ichtiander spent a long time herding together the small and stupid baby dolphins until their mother finally returned and took them to another bay. It took many days to restore their friendship and trust.

***

Christo was becoming seriously worried.

Ichtiander was gone for three days. He returned tired and pale, but pleased with himself.

"Where have you been?" the Indian asked sternly, although he was glad of Ichtiander's return.

"At the bottom," Ichtiander replied.

"Why are you so pale?"

"I... I almost died," Ichtiander lied for the first time in his life and told Christo about an incident that actually took place a long time before.

Deep in the ocean there was a rocky plateau, and above, in the middle of the plateau there was a large oval hollow – an underwater mountain lake.

Ichtiander was swimming above this lake. He was struck by the unusual pale-gray color of the ocean floor. Having gone lower and taken a closer look, Ichtiander was amazed – there was a veritable cemetery of various sea creatures, from small fish to sharks and dolphins. Some of the victims were fairly recent. But they weren't swarmed with small predators – crabs and fish as usual. Everything was dead and motionless. Here and there bubbles of gas rose from the bottom. Ichtiander was swimming above the edge of the hollow. He went lower, and suddenly felt sharp pain in his gills, suffocation and dizziness. Barely conscious, he fell and landed on the edge of the hollow. His temples were thudding, his heart was pounding, red fog obscured his vision. There was no one to ask for help. Suddenly, he saw a shark falling next to him and convulsing. It must have been hunting him before it too became trapped in these terrible, deadly poisonous waters of the underwater lake. Its belly and sides were rising and falling, its mouth was open revealing the chiseled white of its teeth. The shark was dying. Ichtiander shuddered. Clenching his jaws and trying not to inhale with his gills, Ichtiander crawled out of the lake onto the edge, then rose and walked. He became dizzy and fell down again. He pushed away from the gray stones, pulled with his arms and propelled himself thirty feet away from the lake.

Having finished the story, Ichtiander added something he found out from Salvator. "That hollow must have trapped some harmful gases, like hydrogen sulfite or carbon dioxide," Ichtiander said. "You see, at the surface, these gases become oxidized and you don't feel them. But in that hollow, they were highly concentrated. I want some breakfast now, I am hungry."

Having had a hasty breakfast, Ichtiander put on his glasses and gloves and went to the door.

"Is that all you came for?" Christo said, pointing at the glasses. "Why don't you tell me what's wrong with you?"

A new trait formed in Ichtiander's character – he was becoming secretive.

64

"Don't ask me, Christo, I myself don't know what's wrong with me." And the young man quickly left the room.

A SMALL REVENGE

Having unexpectedly met the blue-eyed girl in the shop of Balthazar the pearl seller, Ichtiander was so taken aback that he ran out of the shop and toward the sea. Now he wanted to see the girl again, but he didn't know how to do that. The easiest way would be to ask Christo for help and go with him. But he didn't want to meet with her in front of Christo. Every day Ichtiander went to the shore where he first saw the girl. He stayed there from morning until evening, hiding behind the rocks in hopes of seeing her. When he came on land, he took off his glasses and gloves and put on the white suit to keep from scaring the girl. Sometimes, he stayed there overnight, returning to the sea after dark, eating fish and oysters, and getting a few hours of troubled sleep, only to return to his post early in the morning, before sunrise.

One evening he dared to go to the pearl seller's shop. The door was open, but it was the old Indian sitting by the counter – the girl wasn't there. Ichtiander returned to the shore.

He found the girl standing on the rocky shore, dressed in a light white dress and a straw hat. Ichtiander halted, uncertain whether to approach her. The girl was waiting for someone. She walked back and forth impatiently, glancing at the road from time to time. She did not notice Ichtiander who hid behind a rocky overhang.

Suddenly, the girl waved at someone. Ichtiander glanced back and saw a tall, broad-shouldered young man walking swiftly down the road. Ichtiander had never seen anyone with eyes and hair as light as this stranger's. The giant walked up to the girl, held out his hand, and said gently, "Hello, Gutierre!"

"Hello, Olsen!" she replied. The stranger firmly shook Gutierre's small hand. Ichtiander watched them with some animosity. He suddenly felt sad and could barely keep from crying.

"Is this it?" the giant asked pointing at Gutierre's pearl necklace.

She nodded.

"Won't your father look for it?" Olsen asked.

"No," the girl replied. "These pearls belong to me, and I can do with them as I wish."

Gutierre and Olsen walked to the very edge of the rocky drop, talking quietly. The Gutierre unclasped the pearl necklace, picked it up by the end, raised her hand and said, admiring the pearls, "Look how pretty the pearls are in the sunset light. Take it, Olsen."

Olsen held out his hand, but the necklace suddenly slipped from Gutierre's hand and fell into the sea.

"What have I done!" the girl exclaimed.

Olsen and Gutierre gazed down, both of them upset.

"Perhaps, we can still get it?" Olsen said.

"The ocean is very deep here," Gutierre said and added. "I am so sorry, Olsen!"

Ichtiander saw that the girl was distraught. He immediately forgot that she intended to give her pearls to the fair-haired giant. Ichtiander could not remain indifferent to her plight – he stepped out from behind the rock and walked up to Gutierre.

Olsen frowned, and Gutierre looked at Ichtiander with curiosity and surprise – she recognized him as the young man who ran away from the shop so suddenly.

"I believe you dropped your pearl necklace into the sea?" Ichtiander asked. "If you would like, I can get it for you."

"Even my father – the best pearl diver – couldn't get it at this depth," the girl objected.

"I shall try," Ichtiander replied modestly. To the surprise of Gutierre and her companion, he dove directly into the sea from the tall cliff, still dressed in his suit, and vanished in the waves. Olsen didn't know what to think.

"Who is that? Where did he come from?"

A minute passed, then another one, but the boy still wasn't back.

"He's gone," Gutierre said anxiously, gazing at the waves. Ichtiander didn't want the girl to know that he could live underwater. He became so absorbed in the search and spent somewhat longer time underwater than was normal for a diver. He surfaced and said with a smile, "A little patience. There are many broken rocks at the bottom – they make it hard to search. But I'll find it." And he dove again.

Gutierre had been present during pearl diving many times. She was surprised that the young man, who spent nearly two minutes underwater, was breathing normally and did not appear tired.

Two minutes later, Ichtiander's head appeared above the surface once again. His face shone with joy. He raised his arms above water, clasping the necklace.

"It was caught on a rock," Ichtiander said in a completely even voice, without any gasping, as if he had just walked in from the next room. "Had it fallen into a crack, this would have taken longer."

He quickly climbed the rocks, walked up to Gutierre and gave her the necklace. Water was streaming down his clothes, but he paid no attention.

"Take it."

"Thank you," Gutierre said, looking at the young man with renewed curiosity.

A silence followed. None of them knew what to do next. Gutierre didn't dare give the necklace to Olsen in front of Ichtiander.

"I thought you wanted to give the necklace to him," Ichtiander said, pointing at Olsen.

Olsen blushed, and Gutierre said awkwardly, "Yes, yes," and held the necklace out to Olsen, who took it silently and put it into his pocket.

Ichtiander was pleased. This was a small revenge on his part. The giant received the lost pearls from Gutierre, but also from him — Ichtiander.

He bowed to the girl and swiftly walked away.

Ichtiander wasn't happy about his success for very long. New thoughts and questions roiled in his head. He knew people poorly. Who was this blond giant? Why did Gutierre give him her necklace? What were they talking about?

That night, Ichtiander once again raced around on his dolphin, frightening the fishermen with his screams.

Ichtiander spent the entire next day underwater. He wore his glasses but not his gloves. He crawled over the ocean floor looking for pearl oysters. In the evening he visited Christo, who met him with grumbling reproach. In the morning, fully dressed, he was back by the rock where he ran into Gutierre and Olsen the previous time. In the evening, at sunset, Gutierre appeared first.

Ichtiander stepped out from behind the rock and walked up to the girl. When she saw him, Gutierre nodded to him as a friend, and asked with a smile, "Are you following me?"

"Yes," Ichtiander replied simply, "ever since I first saw you." The young man continued somewhat awkwardly, "You gave your necklace to him... Olsen. But you admired your pearls before you gave them away. Do you like pearls?"

"Yes."

"Then take this. From me." He held out a pearl.

Gutierre was very familiar with the value of pearls. The one that rested in Ichtiander's hand surpassed everything she had ever seen and known about pearls based on what her father told her. The enormous, flawlessly round pearl of pristine white color weighed no less than two hundred carats and was probably worth no less than a million golden pesos. Gutierre stared at the incredible pearl and at the handsome young man before her in astonishment. Strong, agile, healthy, a little shy, dressed in a rumpled white suit, he didn't look like the wealthy young men of Buenos Aires. Yet here he was, offering her, the girl he barely knew, a gift like that.

"Take it," Ichtiander repeated insistently.

"No," Gutierre replied, shaking her head. "I cannot accept such a valuable gift from you."

"It's not all that valuable," Ichtiander objected heatedly. "There are thousands of pearls like this at the ocean floor."

Gutierre smiled. Ichtiander was taken aback. He blushed and added after a brief pause, "Please."

"No."

Ichtiander frowned – he was offended.

"If you don't want to take it for yourself," he insisted, "then take it for him, for Olsen. He won't say no."

Gutierre became angry.

"He did not take it for himself," she replied sternly. "You don't know anything."

"Then no?"

"No."

Then Ichtiander threw the pearl far into the sea, nodded silently, turned around and walked away.

This action shocked Gutierre. She stood there, unable to move. To throw a fortune into the sea, as if it were a pebble! She felt embarrassed. Why did she upset this strange young man?"

"Wait, where are you going?"

Ichtiander kept walking, his head low. Gutierre caught up with him, took his hands and looked into his face. Tears were running down the young man's cheeks. He has never cried before, and was wondering why

69

everything looked so foggy and vague, as if he was swimming underwater without glasses.

"Forgive me for upsetting you," the girl said, holding his hands.

ZURITA'S IMPATIENCE

After this meeting, Ichtiander came to the shore not far from the city every evening, found the hidden suit, got dressed and went to the rock to meet Gutierre. They walked along the shore and talked endlessly.

Who was Gutierre's new friend? She could not tell. He was intelligent and witty, he knew many things Gutierre did not know, but at the same time, he knew nothing of simple things known to any city boy. What was the reason for that? Ichtiander spoke about himself reluctantly. He didn't want to tell the truth. All the girl knew about him was that Ichtiander was the son of a doctor, apparently a very wealthy man. He brought up the boy far from the city and from other people and gave him a very unique and one-sided education.

Sometimes they stayed on the shore until darkness. Surf rustled at their feet. Stars flickered above. Their conversation waned. Ichtiander was happy.

"It's time to go," the girl said.

Ichtiander rose reluctantly, walked her to the outskirts of the city, then quickly returned, took off his suit and swam home.

In the morning, after breakfast, he took a large piece of white bread and went to the bay. Sitting at the bottom he fed the bread to the fish. They came up to him, swarmed all around, slipped between his hands and greedily snatched the soggy bread from his hands. Sometimes larger fish burst into this swarm and chased the small ones. Ichtiander rose and chased the predators away with his hands, the small fish hiding behind his back.

He started collecting pearls and putting them away in an underwater grotto. He worked with enthusiasm and soon gathered an entire pile of prime-quality pearls.

Without knowing it, he was becoming the wealthiest man in Argentina, possibly in all of South America. If he wanted to, he could become the richest man in the world. But he gave no thoughts to wealth.

Days passed peacefully. Ichtiander's only regret was that Gutierre lived in the dusty, stuffy, noisy city. If only she too could live underwater, away from the noise and other people! How wonderful that would be! He would have shown her the strange new world, the beautiful underwater flowers. But Gutierre could not live underwater. And he could not live on land. As it was, he was spending too much time there. This was not without consequence – his sides hurt more and more frequently, whenever he spent the time with the girl. But even when his pain became intolerable, he remained with her until she was ready to leave. Another thing bothered Ichtiander – what was it that Gutierre discussed with the blond giant? Ichtiander kept wanting to ask Gutierre, but was afraid to offend her.

One evening the girl told Ichtiander that she would not be there the next evening.

"Why?" he asked with a frown.

"I am busy."

"With what?"

"You mustn't be so curious," the girl replied with a smile. "No need to see me off," she added and left.

Ichtiander returned to the sea. He spent all night stretched out on mossy rocks. He was unhappy. At dawn, he headed home.

Not far from the bay he saw a group of fishermen shooting dolphins. A bullet struck a large dolphin, who jumped high above the water, then dropped down heavily.

"Leading!" Ichtiander exclaimed in horror.

One of the fishermen jumped out of the boat and waited for the wounded animal to surface. But the dolphin surfaced almost three hundred feet away from the poacher, gasped, and dove under again.

The fisherman swam swiftly toward the dolphin. Ichtiander rushed to help his friend. The dolphin surfaced once again, and the fisherman grabbed him by the fin and dragged the weakened animal to the boat.

Ichtiander swam underwater, caught up with the fisherman, and bit him on the leg. The fisherman, thinking he was being attacked by a shark, started kicking with his legs. As he defended himself, the fisherman sliced with his knife at random. The knife skimmed Ichtiander's neck, which was not protected by the scales. Ichtiander let go of the fisherman's leg, and the latter quickly returned to the boat. The dolphin and Ichtiander, both wounded, headed to the bay. The man ordered the dolphin to follow him, and dove into the underwater cavern. The cave was only half-filled with water. Air came in through cracks in the rocks. The dolphin could catch his breath in safety. Ichtiander examined his wound. It wasn't dangerous. The bullet pierced the skin and got stuck in a layer of fat. Ichtiander managed to pull it out with his fingers. The dolphin handled it patiently.

"It will heal," Ichtiander said, gently patting his friend's back.

Now it was time to think of himself. Ichtiander quickly followed the underwater tunnel, came up to the garden and entered the white cottage. Christo became scared when he saw that his charge has been wounded.

"What happened to you?"

"I was wounded by the fishermen when I was defending my dolphin," Ichtiander said.

But Christo didn't believe him.

"Did you go to the city without me again?" he asked suspiciously, binding the wound. Ichtiander said nothing.

"Lift your scales," Christo said and pushed the scales off Ichtiander's shoulder.

The Indian noticed a reddish spot. The sight of it frightened Christo.

"Did they hit you with an oar?" he asked, examining the shoulder. But there was no swelling. Thus must have been a birth mark.

"No," Ichtiander replied.

The boy went to rest in his room, and the old Indian rested his head on his head and thought. He sat there thinking for a long time, then rose and left.

Christo headed toward the city, came to Balthazar's shop, gave Gutierre a suspicious glance and asked, "Is your father home?"

"There," the girl replied, nodding at the door to the next room.

Christo entered the laboratory and closed the door. He found his brother with the beakers, rinsing the pearls. Balthazar was as irritated as he was the last time.

"You are driving me mad!" Balthazar grumbled. "Zurita is mad why you haven't brought the Sea Devil yet. Gutierre disappears every day. She won't even hear about Zurita. She keeps saying, 'No!' Zurita says, 'I am sick of waiting. I'll kidnap her. She'll cry a bit, and then it will all be over.' He is capable of anything."

Christo listened to his brother's complaints and said, "Listen, I can't bring you the Sea Devil because he, like Gutierre, often leaves home without me and disappears for days on end. He doesn't want to go to the city with me. He stopped listening to me. The doctor will scold me for not looking after him better."

"Then we should capture or kidnap Ichtiander as soon as possible, and then you can leave Salvator before he returns, and..."

73

"Wait, Balthazar. Don't interrupt me, brother. We mustn't rush matters with Ichtiander."

"Why not?"

Christo sighed, as if hesitant about sharing his plan.

"You see…" he began.

But at that moment someone entered the shop, and they heard Zurita's loud voice.

"There he is," Balthazar mumbled, throwing the pearls into a tub, "again!"

The door banged open, and Zurita entered the lab.

"Ah, both brothers are here. How long are you going to be wasting my time?" he asked looking between Balthazar and Christo. Christo rose and said with a pleasant smile, "I am doing all I can. Patience. The Sea Devil is not just some little fish. You can't just pull him out. I managed to bring him here once – but you weren't here. The Devil saw the city, didn't like it, and now he doesn't want to come here."

"If he doesn't want to he doesn't have to. I am sick of waiting. I decided to kill two birds with one stone this week. Is Salvator back yet?"

"We expect him any day now."

"We must hurry then. Expect visitors. I have picked some reliable people. You shall open the door to us, Christo, and we'll do the rest. I will let Balthazar know when everything is ready." He turned to Balthazar and said, "As for you, I shall see you tomorrow. But remember, this is the last discussion we are going to have."

The two brothers bowed to him silently. When Zurita turned his back on them, pleasant smiles vanished from the Indians' faces. Balthazar cursed quietly. Christo was thinking about something.

Back at the shop, Zurita was quietly saying something to Gutierre.

"No!" the brothers heard Gutierre's reply. Balthazar shook his head in dismay.

"Christo!" Zurita called. "Come with me, I shall need you today."

AN UNPLEASANT MEETING

Ichtiander was feeling very poorly. The wound on his neck hurt. He had a fever. He was having trouble breathing regular air.

But in the morning, despite his discomfort, he set out to the rocky shore to meet with Gutierre. She arrived at noon.

It was incredibly hot. Ichtiander was suffocating from the scorching air and fine white dust. He wanted to stay on the beach, but Gutierre was in a hurry and had to return to the city.

"My father is leaving on business, and I have to stay at the shop."

"Then I shall see you off," the young man said, and they walked down the sloping dusty road leading to the city.

Partway there, they saw Olsen. He was preoccupied with something and passed by them without noticing Gutierre. But the girl called out to him.

"I only need to say a couple of things to him," Gutierre said to Ichtiander, then turned back and walked over to Olsen.

They spoke about something quietly and quickly. The girl seemed to be reasoning with him.

Ichtiander was walking a few steps behind them.

"Very well, tonight after midnight," he heard Olsen's voice. The giant shook the girl's hand, nodded and walked away.

When Gutierre returned to Ichtiander, her cheeks and ears were burning red. He wanted to finally ask Gutierre about Olsen, but could not think of the right words.

"I can't," he said, gasping, "I must know... Olsen... You are keeping a secret from me. You are meeting him at night. Do you love him?"

Gutierre took Ichtiander's hand, looked at him gently and asked him with a smile, "Do you trust me?"

"I do. You know that I love you," Ichtiander now knew this word. "But I... this is so difficult."

This was true. Ichtiander suffered from the secrets, but at that moment, he was also feeling the acute cutting pain in his sides. He was gasping for breath. Color was gone from his cheeks and his face was completely pale.

"You are very sick," the girl said anxiously. "Please, calm down. My dear boy. I didn't want to tell you everything, but I will, just to calm you down. Listen."

A horseman rode by them, but having glanced at Gutierre, turned his horse and rode up to them. Ichtiander saw a swarthy middle-aged man with bushy mustache and a small goatee.

Somewhere, at some point, Ichtiander had seen this man. In the city? No. It was there, on the shore.

The rider knocked his whip against his boot, looked Ichtiander over with suspicion and disdain and held out a hand to Gutierre.

Having caught her, he suddenly lifted the girl to the saddle, kissed her hand and laughed.

"I got you!" When Gutierre frowned, he let go of her hand and continued mockingly as well as irately, "Since when is it acceptable for a bride to walk around with a strange young man before her wedding?"

Gutierre was getting angry, but he didn't let her speak, "Your father has been waiting for you. I will be at the shop in an hour." Ichtiander did not hear him. He suddenly felt the world grow dark around him, his throat close and his breath stop. He could no longer remain on land.

"You deceived me... after all..." he said with bluish lips.

He wanted to say more to express the full magnitude of his grief or to find out the way things stood, but the pain in his sides was intolerable, and he was feeling faint.

Ichtiander ran off, reached the edge and jumped into the sea.

Gutierre shrieked and staggered. She then ran to Pedro Zurita, "Quick... Save him!"

But Zurita didn't move.

"It is not my habit to keep other people from drowning themselves, when they wish to do so," he said.

Gutierre ran to the shore to dive after Ichtiander. But Zurita kicked his horse, caught up with the girl, grabbed her, set her in the saddle in front of him and rode off.

"I don't interfere with others, as long as the others don't interfere with me. That's better! Come now, Gutierre!"

But Gutierre said nothing. She fainted. She recovered only when they reached her father's shop.

"Who was that young man?" Pedro asked.

Gutierre looked at Zurita with obvious rage and said, "Let me go."

Zurita frowned. *"Nonsense,"* he thought. *"Her romantic hero threw himself into the sea. Just as well."* Zurita turned toward the shop and shouted, "Father! Balthazar! Hey!"

Balthazar ran out.

"Here is your daughter. You should thank me. I saved her. She almost threw herself into the sea to follow a young man of rather pleasant appearance. This is the second time I saved your daughter's life and she still doesn't like me. But soon, this stubbornness will come to an end." He laughed. "I shall be back in an hour. Remember our agreement!"

Balthazar bowed humbly receiving his daughter from Pedro.

The horseman kicked his horse and rode off.

Father and daughter entered the shop. Gutierre dropped onto a chair helplessly and covered her face.

Balthazar closed the door and started pacing around the shop and speaking about something with much agitation. But no one was listening to him. Balthazar may as well have lectured the dried crabs and blowfish on the shelves.

"He drowned himself," the girl thought remembering Ichtiander's face. "Poor boy! First Olsen, then this ridiculous meeting with Zurita. How dare he call me a bride! It's all over now..."

Gutierre started crying.

She missed Ichtiander. So shy and unassuming – there was no comparing him with the arrogant and careless young men of Buenos Aires.

"What am I going to do?" she thought. "Dive into the sea, like Ichtiander? Kill myself?"

Balthazar kept talking and talking, "Do you understand, Gutierre? We are completely bankrupt. Everything you see in our shop belongs to Zurita. Not even a tenth of it is mine. We get the pearls as my commission from Zurita. But if you refuse him again, he will take everything away and never work with me again. And I'll be ruined! Completely ruined! Please, be a good girl, take pity on your old father..."

"And marry him? No!" Gutierre replied abruptly.

"Damnation!" Balthazar screamed in rage. "If that is your answer, then... then... I will let Zurita deal with you!" And the old Indian went into the laboratory and slammed the door.

A BATTLE WITH SQUIDS

After he dove into the sea, Ichtiander temporarily forgot his landside troubles. After the hot and stuffy land, the cool water refreshed and calmed him down. The stabbing pain went away. He was breathing deeply and evenly. He needed to rest and try not to think about what happened on the shore.

Ichtiander wanted to work, to move. What could he do? Late at night, he loved to dive from a tall cliff and see if he could reach the ocean floor in one leap. But it was noon, and the sea was scattered with the black keels of fishing boats.

"Here is what I'll do. I shall clean out the grotto," Ichtiander thought. In a sheer wall of the bay there was a grotto with a large archway offering a beautiful view of an underwater valley, sloping gently deep into the ocean.

Ichtiander have long since wanted this grotto for himself. But before he could move in, he had to get rid of the long-time tenants of the grotto – the numerous families of squids.

Ichtiander put on his glasses, armed himself with the long, sharp, slightly curved knife, and bravely swam toward the grotto. He was a little hesitant to enter the grotto, and Ichtiander decided to lure his enemies outside. Some time ago, he had noticed a long gaff next to a sunken boat. He picked it up and, standing by the entrance to the grotto, started moving it back and forth. The squids, unhappy about the intrusion, started moving. Long undulating tentacles appeared by the sides of the archway. They carefully approached the gaff. Ichtiander pulled the gaff back before the tentacles managed to grab it. This game continued several minutes. Dozens of tentacles moved around the archway, like Medusa's hair. Finally, an enormous old squid lost his patience and decided to do away with the insolent newcomer. The squid crawled out of the opening, his tentacles moving menacingly. He slowly swam toward his opponent, changing his color to intimidate Ichtiander. Ichtiander moved to the side, threw down the gaff and prepared to fight. Ichtiander knew how difficult it would be for him to work with two arms, when his adversary had eight. He might cut off one tentacle, but at the same time the remaining seven could grab him and trap his arms. He wanted to strike with his knife directly at the squid's body. Letting the monster get close enough to reach

78

him with the tips of the tentacles, Ichtiander suddenly dashed forward, into the center of the undulating limbs, toward the squid's head.

This unusual technique always caught squids by surprise. It took at least four seconds for the animal to draw in all of the tentacles and wrap them around the enemy. In that time, Ichtiander managed to slice the squid's body in half, strike the heart and cut the nerves responsible for the motor functions. The enormous tentacles already wrapped round his body suddenly sagged and drooped.

"One is finished!"

Ichtiander once again picked up the gaff. This time, two squids came at him simultaneously. One of them swam straight at Ichtiander, while the other circled around and tried attacking him from behind. This was becoming dangerous. Ichtiander bravely attacked the squid in front of him, but before he managed to kill him, the second squid wrapped around his neck from behind. The man quickly cut the squid's tentacle, piercing it with the knife right next to his own neck. He then turned to face the squid and cut off the other tentacles. The crippled squid dropped to the bottom, rocking slowly. In the meantime, Ichtiander did away with the squid that attacked him from the front.

"Three," Ichtiander kept counting. He had to stop the battle for a bit. An entire group of squids emerged from the grotto, but the spilled blood muddled the water. Squids would have the advantage in this brown muck, because they could find the enemy by touch, while Ichtiander could not see them. He swam away from the battle field, where water was clear, and took down another squid emerging from the cloud of blood.

The battle continued on and off for several hours.

When the last squid was dead and the water cleared, Ichtiander saw that the ocean floor around him was covered with dead squid bodies and moving tentacles. Ichtiander entered the grotto. There were still a few small squids left there. They were as big as a human fist, with tentacles no thicker than a finger. Ichtiander wanted to kill them too, but felt sorry for them. "*I should try taming them. It wouldn't be a bad idea to have such sentinels.*"

Having cleared the grotto of the large squids, Ichtiander decided to furnish his new dwelling. He brought a metal table with marble top from home and two Chinese vases. He put the table in the middle of the grotto, placed the vases on top of it, poured some sand into the vases and planted some sea plants in them. The sand got washed up by the water and hung above the vases like smoke for a while, but settled down eventually. Only the flowers, moved by the water, rocked slightly as if in the wind.

There was a ledge by the side of the cave, like a natural stone bench. The new master of the grotto happily stretched on it. Even though it was stone, he could barely feel it in the water.

It was a strange underwater room with Chinese vases on the table. Many curious fish showed up to take a peek at this strange homecoming. They darted between the legs of the table, came up to the flowers in the vases, as if to smell them, and swarmed around Ichtiander's head. A marble goby glanced into the grotto, flipped its tail in fright and swam away. A large crab crept in across the white sand, raised and lowered its pincer, as if greeting the host, and then settled under the table.

Ichtiander was amused by this idea. "How else can I decorate my abode?" he thought. "I shall plant the prettiest underwater plants by the entrance, cover the floor with pearls and make a border of seashells by the walls. If only Gutierre could see this room. But she deceived me. Or maybe she didn't. She never got a chance to tell me about Olsen." Ichtiander frowned. As soon as he stopped working, he once again felt lonely and isolated from other people. "Why can't anyone else live underwater? Just me. I wish father would come back! I shall ask him..."

He wanted to show his new underwater dwelling to at least one living creature. "*Leading,*" Ichtiander remembered the dolphin. He found a spiral seashell, surfaced and trumpeted. Soon he heard the familiar snorting – the dolphin always kept close to the bay.

When the dolphin arrived, Ichtiander wrapped around him gently and said, "Come visit me, Leading, I will show you a new room. You have never seen a table or Chinese vases."

Ichtiander dove and gestured to the dolphin to follow.

But the dolphin turned out to be a very troublesome guest. Big and unwieldy, he caused so much water movement in the grotto that the vases rocked back and forth on the table. He also managed to nudge the table with his nose and overturn it. The vases fell, and had they been on solid ground, they would have shattered. But here, they were safe, and all was well, aside from the frightened crab who quickly ran off to the wall sideways.

"*You are so clumsy!*" Ichtiander thought about his friend, moving the table further into the grotto and picking up the vases.

Hugging the dolphin once again, Ichtiander continued talking to him, "Stay here with me, Leading."

But the dolphin soon started shaking his head and showing discomfort. He could not remain underwater very long. He needed air. With a movement of his flippers, the dolphin swam out of the grotto and rose to the surface.

"Even Leading can't live underwater with me," Ichtiander thought sadly once he was alone. "Only the fish. But they are stupid and furtive…"

He settled back on his stone bench. Sun had set. The grotto grew dark. The light movement of the water made Ichtiander sleepy.

Tired from the tribulation of his day and all the work, Ichtiander dozed off.

A NEW FRIEND

Olsen was sitting in a large longboat gazing in the water. The sun has only just risen above the horizon, and its slanting rays lit up the small transparent bay all the way to the bottom. Several Indians were crawling over the white sandy ocean floor. From time to time they surfaced to catch their breath, then dove again. Olsen watched the divers. Despite the early hour it was already hot. "*Should I freshen up and take a couple of dives?*" he thought, quickly undressed and jumped into the water. Olsen had never done any diving and he was surprised to discover he enjoyed it. He realized he could spend more time underwater than the trained divers. Olsen joined the divers and soon became absorbed in this new task.

When he dove the third time, he noticed that two Indians kneeling on the ocean floor, suddenly jumped up and surfaced so quickly as if they were chased by a shark or a sawfish. Olsen glanced around. A strange creature was swimming quickly toward him, half-man/half-frog, with silvery scales, enormous bulging eyes, and frog feet. It was swimming like a frog, kicking out with its legs and swiftly propelling itself forward.

Before Olsen managed to rise, the monster was next to him and grabbed his hand with its frog paw. As frightened as he was, Olsen noticed that the creature had an attractive human face, ruined only by the enormous sparkling eyes. The strange creature, forgetting they were underwater, started saying something. Olsen could not hear the words and only saw the moving lips. The strange creature kept firmly holding Olsen's hand with its paws. Olsen pushed hard with his legs and quickly rose to the surface, using his free arm to keep himself afloat. The monster followed him, still holding on. When they surfaced, Olsen grabbed the side of the longboat, swung one leg over, climbed in, and pushed away this half-human with frog hands so hard that he fell back into the water. The Indians sitting in the longboat jumped off and quickly swam toward the shore.

Ichtiander once again approached the longboat and said to Olsen in Spanish, "Listen, Olsen, I must speak to you about Gutierre."

These words astonished Olsen as much as the underwater meeting. Olsen was a brave and sensible man. If the strange creature knew his name and Gutierre's, then he must be a person and not a monster.

"I am listening," Olsen replied.

Ichtiander climbed into the longboat, settled down at the bow, folding his legs and crossing his arms at his chest.

"*Glasses!*" Olsen thought, looking carefully at the stranger's bulging glittering eyes.

"My name is Ichtiander. One time, I found a necklace for you at the bottom of the sea."

"But then you had human eyes and hands." Ichtiander smiled and shook his frog hands.

"These come off," he said.

"That's what I thought."

The Indians watched this strange conversation curiously from behind the rocks, even though they could not hear the words.

"Do you love Gutierre?" Ichtiander asked after a brief pause.

"Yes, I do," Olsen replied simply. Ichtiander sighed heavily.

"Does she love you too?"

"She does."

"But I thought she loved me."

"That is her business." Olsen shrugged.

"What do you mean? She is your fiancée."

Olsen's face showed surprise, and he replied with his former calm, "No, she is not."

"You are lying," Ichtiander said heatedly. "I heard that the dark man on horseman said that she was a bride."

"My bride?"

Ichtiander was taken aback. No, the dark man did not say that Gutierre was Olsen's bride. But how could a young woman be a bride of that dark fellow, so old and unpleasant? How could it be? The dark man had to be her relative. Ichtiander decided to change his line of questioning.

"What are you doing here? Pearl diving?"

"I admit, I don't like your questions," Olsen replied glumly. "Had I not known a thing or two about you from Gutierre, I would have thrown you off the boat and ended this conversation. No need to grab your knife. I can smash your head with an oar before you get on your feet. But there is no need to deny that I really was looking for pearls."

"The big pearl I threw into the sea? Did Gutierre tell you about that?"

Olsen nodded. Ichtiander rejoiced.

"See? I told her you wouldn't refuse the pearl. I offered her to take the pearl and give it to you. She refused, and here you are now, looking for it."

"Yes, because now it belongs to the ocean, and not to you. And so, if I find it, I won't owe anyone."

"Are you so fond of pearls?"

"I am not a woman to be fond of trinkets," Olsen replied.

"But pearls can be… what do they call it? Yes! They can be sold," Ichtiander recalled the word he barely understood, "for a lot of money." Olsen nodded once again.

"Are you fond of money then?"

"What exactly do you want from me?" Olsen asked with some irritation.

"I must know why Gutierre gave you her pearls. Were you going to marry her?"

"No, I was not going to marry Gutierre," Olsen said. "And even if I did, it's too late now. Gutierre is married to someone else."

Ichtiander went pale and grabbed Olsen's hand.

"That dark one?" he asked fearfully.

"Yes, she married Pedro Zurita."

"But she… I thought she loved me," Ichtiander said quietly.

Olsen looked at him with sympathy, lit up a short pipe and said, "Yes, I think so too. But you threw yourself into the sea and drowned before her eyes – at least, that's what she thought."

Ichtiander looked at Olsen with surprise. He never told Gutierre that he could live underwater. It didn't occur to him that the girl could interpret his jump off the cliff as suicide.

"I saw Gutierre last night," Olsen continued. "Your death devastated her. 'Ichtiander's death is my fault,' she said."

"But then why did she marry another man so quickly? She… I saved her life. Yes, yes! I have long since thought that Gutierre looked like a girl that almost drowned in the ocean. I carried her to the beach and hid behind the rocks there. And then the dark man came – I recognized him right away – and told her that he was the one who saved her."

"Gutierre told me about this," Olsen said. "She was never certain who saved her – Zurita or the strange creature that appeared before her when she first came to. Why didn't you tell her it was you?"

"It would have been awkward. Besides, I wasn't sure it was Gutierre until I saw Zurita. But how could she agree?" Ichtiander asked.

"I don't quite understand," Olsen said slowly, "how exactly it happened."

"Tell me what you know," Ichtiander asked.

"I work at the button factory as a seashell inspector. That was where I met Gutierre. She brought the seashells – her father sent her when he was busy. We met and became friends. We sometimes saw each other at the port and went for walks along the beach. She told me her troubles – she was being courted by a wealthy Spaniard."

"That one? Zurita?"

"Yes, Zurita. Gutierre's father, Balthazar, had high hopes for the marriage and kept convincing his daughter not to refuse such an enviable suitor."

"How is he enviable? He's old, disgusting, he smells terrible," Ichtiander couldn't help himself.

"For Balthazar, Zurita would be a great son-in-law. Especially considering that Balthazar owed Zurita a large sum of money. If Gutierre refused to marry him, Zurita could destroy Balthazar's business. Imagine what her life was like. On one hand – Zurita's persistent courting, on the other – the constant reproaches, reprimands, and threats from her father."

"Why didn't Gutierre tell Zurita to go away? And you – you are so big and strong, why didn't you beat him up?"

Olsen smiled but was also surprised – Ichtiander wasn't stupid, but still asked such odd questions. Where did he grow up and who educated him?

"It's not as simple as you think," Olsen replied. "Law, police and courts would stand up to defend Zurita and Balthazar." Ichtiander still looked confused. "Just trust me, it could not be done."

"But then, why didn't she run away?"

"That would have been easier. She wanted to run away, and I promised to help her. I have long since wanted to leave Buenos Aires for North America and I offered Gutierre to come with me."

"Did you want to marry her?" Ichtiander asked.

"You are so pushy," Olsen said, smiling again. "I told you – we were friends. I don't know what might have happened next."

"Then why didn't you leave?"

"Because we didn't have enough money for the trip."

"Does it really cost so much to travel on *Gorrox*?"

"*Gorrox*? *Gorrox* is only for millionaires. It's like you were born yesterday, Ichtiander."

Ichtiander was taken aback, he blushed and decided not to ask any questions that might tell Olsen that he didn't know the most basic things.

"We didn't have enough money even for a third-class ship. There would have been other expenses upon arrival. After all, work is hard to find."

Ichtiander wanted to ask Olsen another question, but restrained himself.

"And then Gutierre decided to sell her pearl necklace."

"If only I knew!" Ichtiander exclaimed, remembering his underwater treasure.

"About what?"

"It's nothing… Please, continue, Olsen."

"We were all ready to go."

"And I… What about me? Forgive me… Then she was going to leave me?"

"This all started before you met. And then, as far as I know, she was going to let you know. She may have even offered you to come with us. She also may have written you from the road if she failed to talk to you beforehand."

"But why with you and not with me? She consulted with you and was going away with you!"

"She has known me for over a year, and you…"

"Keep talking, keep talking, pay no attention to me."

"Well then. It was all set," Olsen continued. "But then you dove into the sea in front of her, after Zurita accidentally ran into you with Gutierre. Early in the morning, before going to the factory, I stopped by to see Gutierre. I have done so in the past. Balthazar treated me fairly well. Maybe he was afraid of my fists, or maybe he saw me as another suitor, should Zurita tire of Gutierre's refusals. In any case, Balthazar never got in our way and only asked to stay away from Zurita. Of course, the old Indian had no idea about our plans. That morning I was going to tell Gutierre that I bought our tickets and that she had to be ready by ten in the evening. Balthazar met me in the doorway, he was very agitated. 'Gutierre is not home. And she… is gone,' Balthazar said. 'Half an hour

86

ago Zurita rode up in a new shiny car. How about that!' Balthazar exclaimed. 'A car is a rarity in our street, especially when it rolls up to this door. Gutierre and I ran out to see what it was. Zurita was standing there with the car door open and offered Gutierre to take her to the market and back. He knew that Gutierre went to the market around that time. Gutierre looked at the shiny car. You understand what a temptation it was for a young girl. But Gutierre is cunning and suspicious. She politely refused. Have you ever seen a girl this stubborn!' Balthazar shouted in anger, but then laughed. 'But Zurita didn't back down. He said she must have been feeling shy and offered to help her. He grabbed her and put her in the car. Gutierre cried out for me, and then they were gone. I don't think she'll be back. Zurita has taken her to his place,' Balthazar finished his story and it was obvious that he was very pleased. 'Your daughter was kidnapped right in front of you, and you are talking about it so calmly, even happily!' I said to him. 'What have I got to worry about?' Balthazar was surprised. 'Had it been someone else, it would have been different, but I've known Zurita for a long time. He is a penny pincher, but still splurged on a car, so he must really like Gutierre. I am sure he'll marry her. Let this be a lesson to her not to be so stubborn. Wealthy suitors are hard to find. Zurita has a hacienda called Dolores, not far from Parana City. His mother lives there. That's probably where he had taken my Gutierre.'."

"Why didn't you beat up Balthazar?" Ichtiander asked.

"According to you, all I should do is get into fights," Olsen replied. "I admit, I wanted to kick him. But then I decided I would only make things worse. I thought not everything was lost yet. I'll spare you the details. As I said, I managed to see Gutierre."

"At hacienda *Dolores*?"

"Yes."

"Why didn't you kill that scoundrel Zurita and free Gutierre?"

"First I have to beat people, and now I have to kill them! Who knew you were so bloodthirsty?"

"I am not bloodthirsty!" Ichtiander exclaimed with tears in his eyes. "But this is outrageous!"

Olsen felt sorry for him.

"You are right, Ichtiander," he said. "Zurita and Balthazar are unscrupulous people, and they deserve nothing but anger and disdain. They deserve a good beating. But life is more complicated than you imagine. Gutierre herself refused to run away from Zurita."

"She did?" Ichtiander couldn't believe it.

"Yes, she did."

"Why?"

"First of all, she is convinced that you have killed yourself – drowned yourself because of her. Your death is depressing her. She must have loved you very much, poor thing. 'My life is over, Olsen,' she said to me. 'I don't want anything. I don't care about anything. I could barely understand what was going on, when the priest Zurita invited was marrying us. The priest said that nothing happened without the will of God, when he put the ring on my finger, and that what God joined no man must pull apart. I will be unhappy with Zurita, but I am afraid of God's wrath, and I shall never leave him.'"

"But this is nonsense! What God? Father says that God is a fairy tale for little kids!" Ichtiander exclaimed heatedly. "Couldn't you convince her?"

"Unfortunately, Gutierre believes this fairy tale. The missionaries managed to turn her into a devout Catholic. I tried but I could never convince her otherwise. She even threatened to break off our friendship, if I brought up God and the church. And so I had to wait. At the hacienda I had no time to argue with her. I only managed to exchange a few words with her. Here is something else. Once they were married, Zurita laughed and said, 'One thing is done! We've caught the little bird and caged her. All we have to do is catch the fish!' He explained to Gutierre, and she told me what he was talking about. Zurita is coming back to Buenos Aires to capture the Sea Devil, and then he would be able to offer Gutierre millions. Are you the Sea Devil by any chance? You can be underwater without any harm, you scare the pearl divers..."

Caution kept Ichtiander from telling his secret to Olsen. He couldn't explain it anyway. Ignoring the question he asked, "What does Zurita want with the Sea Devil?"

"Pedro wants to make him get pearls for him. So, if you are the Sea Devil, be careful!"

"I appreciate the warning," the young man said. Ichtiander had no idea that his pranks were the talk of the entire coast and much discussed in newspapers and magazines.

"I can't," Ichtiander said suddenly, "I must see her. Talk to her at least one last time. Parana City? Yes, I know where that is. Up the river Parana. How do I get from the city to hacienda *Dolores*?"

Olsen explained.

Ichtiander shook his hand, "Forgive me. I thought you to be my enemy, but unexpectedly found a friend. Farewell. I am going to look for Gutierre."

"Now?" Olsen asked with a smile.

"Yes, I haven't a moment to lose," Ichtiander replied, jumped into the water, and swam toward the shore.

Olsen shook his head.

PART TWO

ON THE WAY

Ichtiander quickly got ready. He found the suit and shoes hidden on the beach, and strapped them to his back with his knife belt. He put on his glasses and gloves and set out.

There were many ocean liners, schooners and longboats anchored in the bay Rio de la Plata. Between them darted small steam launches. Seen from underneath, they resembled water beetles moving on the surface in every direction. Anchor chains and cables rose from the bottom like thin trunks of an underwater forest. The bay floor was covered with various trash, scrap metal, piles of spilled coal and slag, bits of old hose, pieces of sails, jugs, bricks, broken bottles, cans, and, closer to the shore, dog and cat corpses.

A thin layer of oil covered the surface. The sun was still up, but the bay was swathed in greenish-gray twilight. The Parana carried in sand and silt, darkening the water in the bay.

Ichtiander might have gotten lost in this labyrinth of ships, but he used a slight current entering the bay as his compass. "*It's amazing how untidy people can be,*" he thought, looking in revulsion at the bay floor resembling a junk yard. He was swimming across the bay just below the ships' keels. He was having difficulty breathing in the bay's polluted waters, as a person would in a stuffy room.

In several places he saw human corpses and animal skeletons. One body had a broken skull and a rope wrapped around its neck, with a stone attached to it. Someone's crime has been buried there. Ichtiander hurried to get out of this gloomy place.

The further he went into the bay, the more he felt the oncoming current. It was becoming difficult to swim. He had encountered ocean currents, of course, but they were helpful and he knew them well. He used them as a sailor might use a good wind. But here, there was nothing but a crosscurrent. Ichtiander was an experienced swimmer, but he was irritated by having to move so slowly.

Something flew by him and almost hit him. An anchor has been dropped off a ship. "*It's not safe here,*" Ichtiander thought and looked around. A large ship was catching up to him.

Ichtiander went lower and when the ship passed above him, he grabbed its keel. Shells covered the metal in a rough mess, which made it easier to hold on. Being stretched out underwater like this was not very comfortable, but at least he was protected and moved along swiftly, carried by the ship.

Having passed the river delta, the ship sailed up the Parana. The river waters carried a tremendous amount of silt. Ichtiander had trouble breathing in it. His arms were numb but he didn't want to let go of the ship. "*It's too bad I couldn't take Leading!*" he thought. But the dolphin could have been killed in the river. Leading couldn't stay underwater the entire way, and Ichtiander was afraid to surface, because of too much traffic.

Ichtiander's arms grew increasingly tired. Besides, he was very hungry, because he didn't have anything to eat all day. He had to stop. He let go of the ship's keep and dropped to the bottom of the river.

The twilight was thickening. Ichtiander looked around the silty river floor. But he didn't find either the flat flounder or the oysters. Fresh water fish darted around him, but he didn't know their habits and they appeared more elusive than the sea fish. They were difficult to catch. Only when the night fell and the fish went to sleep, Ichtiander managed to catch a large pike. Its meat was coarse and smelled like river slime, but he was hungry and ate it with gusto, gobbling up large pieces complete with bones.

He had to rest. At least he could have a good night's sleep in the river, without having to worry about sharks and octopi. But he had to make sure that the current didn't carry him downstream while he slept. Ichtiander found several stones at the bottom, gathered them into a pile and settled down with one arm wrapped around the stones.

He didn't sleep very long. Soon he felt another ship approaching. Ichtiander opened his eyes and saw its signal lights. The ship was traveling upstream. The young man quickly rose and prepared to grab the keel. But it turned out to be a motor boat with a completely smooth bottom. While attempting in vain to hold on to something, Ichtiander almost ended up under its propeller.

Several ships traveled downstream. Finally, Ichtiander managed to attach himself to a passenger ship going upstream.

Ichtiander eventually made it to Parana City. The first part of his trip was over. The part that remained was more difficult because he had to travel on land.

Early in the morning, Ichtiander swam from the noisy city port into a deserted area, carefully looked around and came on shore. He took off his glasses and gloves and buried them in the sand. He dried his suit in the sun and got dressed. His clothes being so rumpled, he looked like a vagrant. But he gave it no thought.

Ichtiander set off along the right bank, as Olsen told him, asking the fishermen he met along the way, how to get to Pedro Zurita's hacienda *Dolores*.

The fishermen looked at him suspiciously and shook their heads.

Hours passed, the heat increased, but his search was still in vain. Ichtiander was completely ignorant of finding his way around on land. The heat was wearing him out, he was dizzy and was having trouble focusing.

In order to cool off, Ichtiander had to stop several times to undress and dive into the river.

Finally, around four in the afternoon, he was fortunate to run into an old peasant, possibly a farmhand. Having listened to Ichtiander, the old man nodded and said, "Follow this road across the fields. When you reach the big pond, cross the bridge, go up a small hill, and there you'll have the mustachioed Donna Dolores."

"Why mustachioed? I thought *Dolores* was a hacienda?"

"It is. But the old mistress of the hacienda is also named Dolores. Dolores is Pedro Zurita's mother. A fat old lady with a mustache. Don't even think of working for her. She'll eat you alive. A real witch. They say Zurita brought home a young wife. She won't last very long with a mother-in-law like that," the talkative peasant said.

"He is talking about Gutierre," Ichtiander thought.

"Is it far?" he asked.

"You'll get there by evening," the old man said, glancing at the sun. Having thanked him, Ichtiander swiftly walked along the road passing by wheat and corn fields. Rigorous walking was making him tired. The road stretched out endlessly like a white ribbon. The fields were replaced by grazing areas with tall thick grass and flocks of sheep.

Ichtiander was exhausted, the stabbing pain in his sides grew stronger. He was thirsty. There wasn't a drop of water anywhere near. "*I hope I get to the pond soon!*" Ichtiander thought. His eyes and cheeks looked sunken in, he was breathing heavily. He was also hungry. But what could he eat here? Far in the distance a flock of sheep grazed under the watchful eye of a shepherd and several dogs. Peach and orange tree branches covered with ripe fruit hung over a stone fence. But this was different from the ocean. Everything was someone else's, everything was split up, fenced, and protected. Only the birds didn't belong to anyone, as they flew around and screeched. But he couldn't catch them. Besides, was it allowed to catch them? What if they too were someone's property after all? It was easy to die of hunger and thirst here, surrounded by pools, gardens, and flocks.

A fat man in a white jacket with shiny buttons, a white cap, and a gun holster on his belt was walking toward Ichtiander, hands behind his back.

"Please tell me, how far is hacienda *Dolores*?" Ichtiander asked. The fat man looked him over suspiciously.

"What do you need? Where are you from?"

"Buenos Aires."

The man in white grew even more suspicious.

"There is someone there I need to see," Ichtiander added.

"Show me your hands," the fat man said.

This request surprised Ichtiander, but he held out his hands, not anticipating anything bad. The fat man pulled out handcuffs from his pocket and quickly snapped them around Ichtiander's wrists.

"Got you," the man with shiny buttons mumbled, then punched Ichtiander in the side and shouted, "Go! I shall take you to *Dolores*."

"Why did you cuff my hands?" Ichtiander asked in confusion, holding out his hands and examining the cuffs.

"No talking!" the fat man shouted sternly. "Come on!"

Ichtiander hung his head and stumbled down the road. At least he wasn't forced to go back. He did not understand what was happening. He didn't know that there had been a murder and a robber at a nearby farm the night before, and the police were looking for the criminals. He also didn't realize that he looked suspicious in his rumpled suit. His indefinite answer about the goal of his trip decided his fate.

The policeman who arrested Ichtiander was taking him to the nearest village in order to send off to Parana City jail.

Ichtiander knew only one thing for certain – he was deprived of his freedom, and this was causing a vexing delay in his trip.

He decided to escape the first chance he got, no matter what.

The fat policeman, pleased with this catch, lit a long cigar. He was walking behind, blowing clouds of smoke at Ichtiander. Ichtiander was suffocating.

"Would you mind not smoking, I am having trouble breathing," he said to his guard.

"Wha-a-at? No smoking? Ha-ha-ha!" the policeman laughed, his entire face gathering into creases. "Aren't we delicate!" He blew another cloud of smoke into the boy's face and shouted, "Go!"

Ichtiander obeyed.

Finally, Ichtiander saw the pond with a narrow bridge and sped up.

"Don't be in such a hurry to see your Dolores!' the fat man shouted.

They walked onto the bridge. When they reached the middle, Ichtiander suddenly leaned over the railing and fell into the water.

The policeman did not expect this from a man with cuffed hands.

But Ichtiander also did not expect what the fat man did next. The policeman jumped into the pond after Ichtiander – he was afraid that the perpetrator might drown. The policeman wanted him alive – a prisoner who drowned with handcuffs on his hands could cause him a lot of trouble. The policeman followed Ichtiander so quickly that he managed to grab his hair and refused to let go. Then Ichtiander risked losing his scalp and pulled the policeman to the bottom. Soon Ichtiander felt the policeman's hand open and let go of his hair. Ichtiander swam several feet away and peeked out of the water to see whether the policeman had surfaced. The latter was splashing at the surface and, seeing Ichtiander's head, shouted, "You'll drown, you rascal! Swim over here!"

"*It's an idea,*" Ichtiander thought and shouted, "Help! I'm drowning…" and descended to the bottom.

He watched from underwater as the policeman looked for him, diving here and there. Finally, apparently having despaired in success, the policeman returned to the shore.

"*He is leaving,*" Ichtiander thought. But the policeman did not leave. He decided to remain with the corpse, until investigative representatives arrived. The fact that his prisoner was at the bottom of the pond changed nothing.

Just then, a peasant was riding across the bridge on a mule loaded with sacks. The policeman ordered the peasant to leave the sacks and take a note to the nearest police station. Things were turning worse for Ichtiander. Besides, the pond was infested with leeches. They kept attaching themselves to him, and he barely managed to pull them off. But he had to do this carefully, to keep from moving the water too much and attracting the policeman's attention.

The peasant returned in half an hour, pointed at the road, loaded his sacks back onto the mule and left in a hurry. In five minutes, three policemen arrived. Two of them were carrying a light boat, and the third one – a boathook and an oar.

They lowered the boat into the water and started looking for the drowned man. Ichtiander was not afraid of the search. It was almost a game – he kept moving from one place to another. The policemen thoroughly examined the bottom of the pond with the boathook, but did not find the corpse.

The policeman who arrested Ichtiander spread his hands in confusion. Ichtiander found it funny. But soon, things changed for the worse. The policemen raised clouds of silt with their boathook. The water grew dark. Now Ichtiander couldn't see anything beyond his reach, and this was dangerous. More importantly, he was having trouble breathing. He couldn't stand it any longer. He groaned, and several bubbles floated from his mouth. What to do? He had to get out of the pond – he had no other choice. He had to get out, no matter the consequences. Of course, they would catch him, possibly beat him, and put him in jail. But he didn't care. Ichtiander stumbled toward the shallow water and raised his head above the surface.

"A-a-a-a-a!" the policeman screamed, jumping off the boat to reach the shore quickly.

"Jesus and Holy Virgin! O-o-o-o!" another one shrieked, falling to the bottom of the boat.

The two policeman on the shore whispered prayers. They grew pale, started shaking with terror, and tried to hide behind each other.

Ichtiander did not expect this and did not understand the reason for their fright right away. He then remembered that the Spanish were very religious and superstitious. Apparently, the policemen imagined they were seeing a dead man. Ichtiander decided to frighten them even more – he bared his teeth, rolled his eyes, and howled in a terrible voice, as he slowly headed for the shore. He reached the road and staggered away, purposely moving in an odd slow gait.

Not a single policeman moved to detain Ichtiander. Superstitious dread and fear of ghosts interfered with their work ethic.

IT'S THE SEA DEVIL!

Pedro Zurita's mother Dolores was a stocky, well-fed old woman with a hooked nose and prominent chin. A thick mustache made her face strange and unappealing. This ornament, rare for a woman, secured her the nickname Mustachioed Dolores.

When her son showed up with a young wife, the old woman looked Gutierre over unceremoniously. First and foremost, Dolores looked for drawbacks. Gutierre's beauty was striking, even though the old woman showed no sign of being impressed by it. But such was Mustachioed Dolores – having thought about it in her kitchen she decided that Gutierre's beauty was the very drawback she'd been looking for.

Once she was alone with her son, the old woman shook her head in disapproval and said, "Pretty! Much too pretty!" and she added with a sigh, "You'll have nothing but trouble with this beauty. Yes. You would have been better off with a Spanish girl." Having pondered some more, she continued, "And she is proud. And her hands are too soft, too delicate, she'll be no good around the house."

"We'll break her in," Pedro replied and became absorbed in accounting books. Dolores yawned and left to the garden to get some fresh air and keep out of her son's way. She liked to dream in the moonlight.

Mimosas filled the garden with their pleasant fragrance.

White lilies shone in the moonlight. The laurel and rubber plant leaves barely moved.

Dolores settled on a bench surrounded by myrtles and succumbed to her dreams – to buy the adjacent plot of land, breed merino sheep, and build a bunch of new barns.

"Oh, damn you!" the old woman shouted angrily, slapping her own cheek. "These mosquitos give you not a moment's peace."

Clouds gradually covered the sky, and the garden grew dark. A pale blue band became more pronounced on the horizon – the glow from the city lights.

Suddenly, Dolores saw a human head appear above the low stone fence. Someone raised hands, encased in handcuffs, and carefully jumped over the wall.

The old woman became frightened. "Some escaped criminal," she decided. She wanted to cry out but couldn't, then tried to get up and run, but her legs refused. As she sat on the bench, she watched the stranger.

The man in handcuffs carefully made it between the shrubs and came to the house, peeking through the windows.

Suddenly – or did she imagine it? – the criminal called out quietly, "Gutierre!"

"So that's what this beauty's all about! That's who she is friends with! This girl might kill my son and me, rob the hacienda, and run off with the criminal," Dolores thought.

The old woman suddenly felt deep hatred toward her daughter-in-law, combined with bitter spite. This gave her strength. She jumped up and ran to the house.

"Quickly," Dolores whispered to her son. "There is an escaped convict in the garden. He was calling Gutierre."

Pedro ran out so quickly, as if the house was on fire, grabbed a shovel left by the garden path, and ran around the house.

There, by the wall, stood a stranger in a dirty, wrinkled suit, with handcuffed hands, looking into the window.

"Damn!" Zurita mumbled and dropped the shovel onto the man's head.

The latter fell to the ground without a single sound.

"Done," Zurita said quietly.

"Done," Dolores said in a tone suggesting that her son had crushed a poisonous scorpion. Zurita gave his mother a questioning look, "What do we do with him?"

"Into the pond," the old woman pointed. "It's deep."

"He'll float up."

"We'll tie a stone to his feet. One moment..."

Dolores ran back and started looking for a sack they could use to wrap around the body. But she dispatched all of the grain sacks to the mill just that morning. She found a pillowcase and a long rope.

"There are no sacks," she said to her son. "Here, put the stones into the pillowcase and tie it with the rope to the handcuffs."

Zurita nodded, hoisted the body onto his shoulders and dragged it to a small pond at the other end of the garden.

"Don't get any blood on yourself," Dolores whispered, hobbling after her son with the pillowcase and the rope.

"You'll wash it off," Pedro replied, nevertheless moving the man's head so that the blood dripped on the ground."

By the pond, Zurita quickly stuffed the pillowcase with stones, tied it to the man's hands, and threw the body into the water.

"I must change." Pedro glanced at the sky. "Looks like rain. By morning, it will wash off the traces of blood on the ground."

"What about the pond? Won't the water turn pink from blood?" Mustachioed Dolores asked.

"No. There are drains in and out of the pond. Oooh, damn you!" Zurita said hoarsely, as he walked to the house and shook his fist at one of the windows.

"So much for beauty!" the old woman whined, following her son.

Gutierre was given her own room in the loft. She could not sleep that night. It was stuffy, and mosquitos were rampant. Her thoughts were depressing. She could not forget Ichtiander or his death. She did not love her husband, and felt nothing but revulsion to her mother-in-law. Yet Gutierre had to coexist with this mustachioed old woman.

That night Gutierre thought she heard Ichtiander's voice. He called her name. There was a noise and quiet voices in the garden. Gutierre decided she was not going to fall asleep after all. She walked out into the garden. The sun wasn't up yet. The garden was surrounded by early morning twilight. The clouds were gone. Plentiful dew glittered in the grass and trees. In a light robe and barefoot, Gutierre walked across the grass. Suddenly, she stopped and started carefully examining the ground. The sand covering the path by her window was stained with blood. A bloodied shovel lay nearby.

A crime took place here last night. Otherwise, where would the blood have come from?

Gutierre followed the blood traces and they led her to the pond.

"*Is this where the evidence of the crime was hidden?*" she thought, peering fearfully into the green water surface.

Ichtiander's face was looking up at her from underwater. The skin on his temple was cut. His face was filled with suffering but also with joy.

Gutierre couldn't take her eyes off the face of the drowned Ichtiander. Was she going mad?

Ichtiander's face rose from the water. It appeared above the surface and rippled the water. Ichtiander held his chained hands to

Gutierre, abandoning all formality as he addressed her, "Gutierre! My darling! Finally, Gutierre, I..." but he didn't finish.

Gutierre grabbed her head and screamed, "Be gone! Go away, miserable ghost! I know that you are dead. Why must you haunt me?"

"No, no, Gutierre, I am not dead," the ghost replied quickly, "I did not drown. Forgive me, I didn't tell you. I don't know why. Don't leave, listen to me. I am alive – here, you can touch my hands."

He held out his chained hands to her. Gutierre was still just looking at him.

"Don't be afraid, I am alive. I can live underwater. I am not like other people. I am the only one who can live underwater. I didn't drown when I jumped into the sea. I jumped because I was having trouble breathing the hot air."

Ichtiander staggered and continued just as hurriedly and incoherently, "I have been looking for you, Gutierre. Last night, when I came to your window, your husband hit me on the head and threw me into the pond. I came to in the water. I managed to get rid of the sack with rocks, but this," Ichtiander pointed at the cuffs, "I don't know how to take this off."

Gutierre was beginning to believe that she was seeing a living person and not a ghost.

"But why are your hands chained?" she asked.

"I'll tell you later. Come with me, Gutierre. We can stay with my father, nobody will find us. And we can live there together. Please take my hands, Gutierre. Olsen said they called me the Sea Devil, but I am a man. Why are you afraid of me?"

Ichtiander came out of the pond covered in slime. Exhausted, he collapsed in the grass.

Gutierre leaned over him and finally took his hand.

"My poor boy," she said.

"What a pleasant surprise!" a mocking voice suddenly said. They looked around and saw Zurita standing nearby. Just like Gutierre, Zurita was unable to sleep that night. He stepped out into the garden having heard Gutierre's cry and heard the entire conversation. When Pedro discovered that he was indeed seeing the Sea Devil, whom he hunted for so long and so unsuccessfully, he was overjoyed and wanted to immediately take Ichtiander to *Medusa*. But having thought about it, he decided to use a different tactic.

"You will not be able to take Gutierre to Doctor Salvator, Ichtiander, because Gutierre is my wife. You are unlikely to be able to return to your father yourself. The police are looking for you."

"But I haven't done anything wrong!" the young man exclaimed.

"The police do not bestow handcuffs on people for no good reason. And if you landed within my grasp, it is my duty to hand you over to the police."

"Will you really do this?" Gutierre asked her husband indignantly.

"I have to do this," Pedro replied shrugging his shoulders.

"What kind of a man," Dolores chimed in, having suddenly appeared out of nowhere, "would release a convict? Why? To encourage this criminal to peek into other people's windows and kidnap other people's wives?"

Gutierre walked up to her husband, took his hands and said gently, "Let him go. Please. I have done no wrong."

Dolores, afraid that her son might yield to his wife, waved her arms and shouted, "Don't listen to her, Pedro!"

"I cannot resist a beautiful woman's plea," Zurita said pleasantly. "I agree.

"You've only just gotten married and you are already under her boot," the old woman grumbled.

"Wait, mother. We shall cut your handcuffs, young man, change you into a decent suit and deliver you to *Medusa*. In Rio de La Plata you can jump off the ship and go wherever you want. But I will release you on one condition – you must forget Gutierre. And you Gutierre, are coming with me. It's safer that way."

"You are a better man than I thought," Gutierre said sincerely.

Zurita curled his mustache, very pleased with himself, and bowed to his wife.

Dolores knew her son well – she quickly guessed that he was planning some sort of trickery. But in order to support his game, she continued grumbling irately, "Bewitched! You'll spend the rest of your life under her thumb!"

101

FULL SPEED AHEAD

"Salvator is coming tomorrow. I was laid up with a fever, and we have much to talk about," Christo said to Balthazar. They were at Balthazar's shop. "Listen, brother, listen carefully and don't interrupt me, otherwise I'll forget what I wanted to say."

Christo paused, gathering his thoughts and continued, "We have worked hard for Zurita. He is wealthier than you and I, but he wants to be wealthier still. He wants to catch the Sea Devil."

Balthazar made a move to speak.

"Be quiet, brother, be quiet, or else I'll forget what I want to say. Zurita wants to have the Sea Devil as his slave. Do you know what the Sea Devil is? He is a treasure. Limitless riches. The Sea Devil can gather pearls at the ocean floor – many beautiful pearls. But the Sea Devil can get more than that. There are many sunken ships down there with great treasure. He can get it for us. For us, I say, not for Zurita. Do you know, brother, that Ichtiander loves Gutierre?"

Balthazar once again wanted to say something, but Christo didn't let him, "Be quiet and listen. I cannot talk when I am interrupted. Yes, Ichtiander loves Gutierre. He couldn't hide it from me. When I found out about it I thought it was very well. Let Ichtiander fall even more in love with Gutierre. He would be a better husband and son-in-law than Zurita. Gutierre loves Ichtiander too. I have watched them without interfering. Let them see each other."

Balthazar sighed but did not interrupt.

"This is not all, brother. Listen. I want to remind you what happened many years ago. About twenty years ago, I accompanied your wife when she was coming home from her family. Remember, she went into the mountains to her mother's funeral. Along the way, your wife died in childbirth. The baby died too. I didn't tell you everything, I didn't want to upset you. I'll tell you now. Your wife died, but the baby was alive, although very weak. It happened in an Indian village. An old lady told me that a great wizard, god Salvator lived nearby."

Balthazar looked up.

"And she advised me to take the baby to Salvator and save him. I followed her advice and took the baby to Salvator. 'Save him,' I said. Salvator took the baby boy, shook his head and said, 'It would be hard,' and took him away. I waited until evening. In the evening a Negro came

102

out and said, 'The baby died.' And I left. So," Christo continued, "Salvator sent his servant to tell me that the baby died. The little boy – your son – had a birthmark. I remember it very well." After a pause Christo continued, "Recently, Ichtiander has been wounded. As I bound his wound, I pulled away the collar of his scale suit and saw a birthmark exactly like your son's."

Balthazar looked at Christo with wide eyes and asked anxiously, "Do you think Ichtiander is my son?"

"Be quiet, brother, be quiet and listen. Yes, that is what I think. I think Salvator lied. Your son didn't die, and Salvator kept him to make him into the Sea Devil."

"O-oh!" Balthazar screamed, beside himself. "How dare he! I will kill Salvator with my own hands."

"Be quiet! Salvator is stronger than you are. Besides, I could be mistaken. It's been twenty years. Anyone can have a birthmark on his neck. Ichtiander might be your son, or maybe not. We have to be careful. Go to Salvator and tell him that Ichtiander is your son. I shall be your witness. You will demand to have your son returned to you. If he doesn't, you can threaten to take him to court for crippling children. He won't like that. If this doesn't work, go to court. And even if we can't prove in court that Ichtiander is your son, then he can marry Gutierre – after all, she is your adopted daughter. You missed your wife and son so much, so I found you that little orphan Gutierre."

Balthazar jumped up. He was pacing around the shop, brushing against the crabs and seashells.

"My son! My son! This is terrible!"

"Why is it terrible?" Christo wondered.

"I didn't interrupt and listened to you carefully, now you must listen to me. While you had a fever, Gutierre married Pedro Zurita."

Christo was struck by the news.

"And Ichtiander, my poor son," Balthazar hung his head. "Ichtiander was captured by Zurita!"

"Impossible," Christo objected.

"Yes, yes. Ichtiander is aboard *Medusa*. This morning Zurita came to see me. He laughed at me, mocked me and cursed at me. He said we were deceiving him. Just think, he caught Ichtiander on his own, without us! Now he won't pay us anything. But I wouldn't take his money anyway. How could I sell my own son?"

Balthazar was desperate. Christo looked at his brother disapprovingly. It was time for decisive actions. But Balthazar was more likely to hurt matters than help. Christo himself didn't really believe in the connection between Ichtiander and Balthazar. It was true that Christo saw a birthmark on the newborn baby. But was it really proof? Having noticed a birthmark on Ichtiander's neck, Christo decided to take advantage of the resemblance and make some profit off it. But how could he know that his story would have such an effect on Balthazar? However, Balthazar's news scared Christo.

"This isn't a time for tears. We must act. Salvator is coming tomorrow morning. Be brave. Wait for me at the pier at sunrise. We must save Ichtiander. But don't tell Salvator that you are Ichtiander's father. Where did Zurita go?"

"He didn't say, but I think north. Zurita has been planning to go to the Panama coast for a long time."

Christo nodded.

"Remember then – tomorrow morning, before dawn, you must be on the shore. Stay there and don't leave, even if you had to wait until evening."

Christo went back. He spent all night thinking about the upcoming meeting with Salvator. He had to somehow defend himself.

Salvator arrived at sunrise. Christo greeted the doctor with the expression of sadness and devotion on his face, "We have trouble. I have warned Ichtiander many times not to swim in the bay."

"What happened?" Salvator asked impatiently.

"He was kidnapped and taken away on a schooner. I…"

Salvator squeezed Christo's shoulder and looked him in the eye. This lasted only a moment, but Christo's face changed under this searching gaze. Salvator frowned, mumbled something, let go of Christo's shoulder and said, "You will give me the details later." Salvator called one of the Negros, said a few words to him in a language Christo didn't know and, turning back to the Indian, said imperiously, "Come with me!"

Without any rest or even changing his clothes after his trip, Salvator left the house and quickly went to the garden. Christo barely kept up with him. By the third wall, two Negros joined them.

"I guarded Ichtiander like a faithful dog," Christo said gasping from swift walking. "I never left his side…"

But Salvator was not listening. The doctor was already by the pool, tapping his foot impatiently as the water drained through the openings.

"Follow me," Salvator ordered again, descending the underground staircase.

Christo and two other servants followed Salvator in complete darkness. Salvator was skipping several steps at a time, as a man well familiar with this underground labyrinth.

Having reached the lowest landing, Salvator did not turn on the switch as he did the first time, but, having run his hand over the wall, opened a door in the right wall and followed another dark hallway. There were no steps here, and Salvator walked even faster, still without turning on the light.

"What if I drop through a trap door and drown in a well?" Christo thought, trying to keep up with Salvator.

They walked for a long time and finally Christo felt the floor sloping down. Sometimes he thought he heard faint splashing of the waves. Finally, they arrived. Salvator stopped and turned on the light. Christo saw that they were in a large, long, water-filled grotto with arching ceiling. This ceiling gradually sloped toward the water surface. In the water, by the edge of the stone floor, Christo saw a small submarine. Salvator, Christo, and the two Negros got in. Salvator turned on the light inside the submarine, one of the men shut the hatch, and the other was already working with the engine. Christo felt the vessel shudder, slowly turn, submerge and move forward. They surfaced in less than two minutes. Salvator and Christo came up onto the bridge. Christo had never been on a submarine before. But this vessel, gliding across the surface of the ocean, would have surprised even experienced ship builders. It was of an unusual design and, apparently, possessed a tremendously powerful engine. Even traveling at partial speed, the boat moved very swiftly.

"Where did Ichtiander's kidnappers go?"

"Along the shore to the north," Christo replied. "May I suggest that we pick up my brother? I have warned him, and he is waiting on the shore."

"What for?"

"Ichtiander was kidnapped by Zurita, the pearl merchant."

"How do you know that?" Salvator asked suspiciously.

"I described the schooner that captured Ichtiander in the bay, and he recognized it as Pedro Zurita's *Medusa*. Zurita must have kidnapped Ichtiander for pearl diving. And my brother Balthazar knows the best diving spots. He will be useful in our search."

Salvator thought about it.

"Very well. We shall take your brother."

Balthazar was waiting at the pier. The boat turned toward the shore. Balthazar frowned as he watched Salvator who took away and disfigured his son. However, the Indian bowed to Salvator politely and swam out to meet the boat.

"Full speed ahead!" Salvator ordered. He remained on the bridge, gazing at the surface of the ocean.

THE UNUSUAL CAPTIVE

Zurita cut open the handcuffs tying Ichtiander's hands, gave him a new suit, and allowed him to pick up his gloves and glasses he hid in the sand by the river. But as soon as the young man stepped onto the deck of *Medusa*, the Indians grabbed him and put him in the hold following Zurita's orders. Zurita made a quick stop in Buenos Aires to restock provisions. He also went to see Balthazar to brag about his success, and then sailed further along the coast in the direction of Rio de Janeiro. He planned to go around the eastern coast of South America and search for pearls in the Caribbean Sea.

He settled Gutierre in the captain's quarters. Zurita assured her that he set Ichtiander free at the Rio de La Plata bay. But this lie was soon uncovered. In the evening Gutierre heard screams and groans from the hold. She recognized Ichtiander's voice. Zurita was on the upper deck at the time. Gutierre tried leaving the room but discovered that the door was locked. Gutierre started pounding the door with her fists, but no one responded.

Zurita, hearing Ichtiander's shouts, cursed, came down from the bridge and descended into the hold with one of his Indian sailors. The hold was extremely stuffy and dark.

"Why are you shouting?" Zurita asked rudely.

"I... I am suffocating," he heard Ichtiander's voice. "I can't live without water. It's so stuffy here. Let me out into the sea. I won't last the night."

Zurita slammed the trapdoor and returned to the deck.

"*I hope he doesn't really suffocate,*" he thought with concern. Ichtiander's death was not at all profitable to him.

Following Zurita's orders, the sailors brought a large barrel into the hold and filled it with water.

"Here is a bath for you," Zurita said to Ichtiander. "Use it! And tomorrow, I'll let you go into the sea."

Ichtiander quickly dove into the barrel. The sailors watched him in confusion. They didn't know yet that the captive held on *Medusa* was the Sea Devil himself.

"Get back on deck!" Zurita shouted.

It was impossible to swim in the barrel or even stand up. Ichtiander had to crouch in order to be submerged in the water. The barrel was once filled with pickled meat. The water became quickly infused with the smell, and Ichtiander felt marginally better than in the stuffy hold.

At the same time, fresh south-eastern wind was blowing above the sea, taking the schooner further to the north.

Zurita spent a long time at the bridge and returned to his room only in the morning. He assumed that his wife was asleep. But she was sitting on a chair by a narrow table, resting her head on her arms. When he entered, Gutierre rose, and in the weak light of the flickering lamp hanging from the ceiling, Zurita saw her pale, frowning face.

"You lied to me," she said dully.

Zurita didn't feel too well under his wife's angry gaze and to cover up his unwilling embarrassment, he assumed a carefree air, curled up his mustache and replied playfully, "Ichtiander opted to remain on *Medusa* to be near you."

"You are lying! You are a revolting, despicable man. I hate you!" Gutierre suddenly snatched up a large knife hanging on the wall and swung it at Zurita.

"Oho!" Zurita said. He quickly grabbed Gutierre's hand and squeezed it so hard that she dropped the knife.

Zurita kicked the knife out of the room, let go of his wife's hand and said, "That's better! You are very agitated. Have a glass of water."

He left the room, locking the door one again, and returned abovedeck.

The east was already turning rosy, and light clouds lit by the sun still hidden beyond the horizon looked like flames. Seagulls were flying above the sea, peering for fish playing at the surface.

The sun had risen. Zurita was still pacing around the deck with his hands clasped behind his back.

"It's alright, I'll manage somehow," he said, thinking about Gutierre. He loudly ordered the sailors to drop the sails. Medusa dropped anchor and rocked steadily on the water.

"Bring me a chain and go get the man from the hold," Zurita instructed. He wanted to try out Ichtiander as a pearl diver as soon as possible.

"Besides, he'll freshen up in the sea," he thought.

Escorted by two Indians, Ichtiander appeared on deck. He looked tired. Ichtiander looked around. He was standing by the mizzen. He was only a few paces away from the railing. Suddenly, Ichtiander dashed forward, ran up to the railing and was ready to jump. But at that moment, Zurita's heavy fist landed on his head. The boy fell onto the deck unconscious.

"No need to rush," Zurita said sanctimoniously. There was a clanging of metal, as a sailor handed Zurita a long thin chain ending in a metal circle.

Zurita put the circle around the unconscious man's waist, locked it and said to the sailors, "Pour some water on his head."

Soon, the young man came to and looked in confusion at the chain he was now wearing.

"You can't just run away from me," Zurita explained. "I will let you down into the sea. You will look for pearl oysters for me. The more pearls you find, the more you can stay in the water. And if you refuse to do this for me, I shall lock you up in the hold and you'll be stuck in the barrel. Do you understand? Do you agree?"

Ichtiander nodded.

He was ready to get all the treasures of the world for Zurita, only to be able to dive into the clear sea water.

Zurita, Ichtiander and the sailors walked up to the railing. Gutierre's room was on the other side – Zurita didn't want her to see Ichtiander chained down.

Ichtiander was lowered into the sea. If only he could rip it apart! But the chain was very strong. Ichtiander surrendered to his fate. He started collecting pearl oyster shells and putting them into a large sack hanging from his belt. The metal band was squeezing his sides and making breathing difficult. Still, Ichtiander felt almost happy after the stuffy hold and the stinky barrel.

The sailors watched the incredible sight in astonishment. Minutes passed, and the man they lowered to the ocean floor showed no signs of needing to return. At first, air bubbles rose to the surface, but then they stopped.

"May the sharks eat me, if there is a bit of air left in his lungs. He must feel like a fish in the water," an old diver said, peering into the water.

They could clearly see the young man crawling on the sand.

"Maybe it's the Sea Devil himself?" another sailor said quietly.

"Whoever he is, Captain Zurita made a nice purchase," the navigator replied. "One such diver is worth a dozen."

It was almost noon, and the sun was high in the sky, when Ichtiander tugged on the chain to be raised. His bag was filled with shells. He needed to empty it in order to continue his search.

The sailors swiftly lifted the unusual diver to the deck. Everyone wanted to know what his catch was like.

Normally, the pearl oysters were left alone for a few days to allow the mollusks to rot and make it easier to extract the pearls, but the impatience of the sailors and Zurita himself was far too great. They started opening the shells with knives.

When the sailors finished working, everyone started talking at once. Everyone on deck was excited. Perhaps, Ichtiander merely found a good spot. However, what he delivered after a single dive surpassed all expectations. Among the shells he brought up there were two dozen very large pearls, flawless in shape and of the most delicate colors. The very first catch secured Zurita an entire fortune. One of these large pearls was enough to buy a new beautiful schooner. Zurita was well on his way to riches. His dreams were coming true.

Zurita saw the greedy looks by the sailors. He didn't like it. He quickly poured the pearls into his straw hat and said, "It's time for lunch. You are a good diver, Ichtiander. I have a spare room. You will stay there. It won't be so stuffy. And I'll order a large cistern for you. Maybe you won't even need it, now that you can swim in the sea every day. I know you don't like the chain, but what choice do I have? Otherwise, you'll dive down to your crabs and won't come back."

Ichtiander didn't want to talk to Zurita. But now that he was a prisoner of this greedy man, he may as well consider better living conditions.

"A cistern would be better than the stinky barrel," he said to Zurita, "but in order for me to breathe, you'll have to change water in it."

"How often?"

"Every half hour," Ichtiander replied. "It would be even better if water was circulated continuously."

"Hey, I see you start taking on airs. I praised you once, and you are already getting picky."

"I am not picky," the young man was offended. "I... Please understand, if you put a large fish into a bucket, it will soon fall asleep. The fish breathes oxygen in the water and I am just a really big fish," Ichtiander added with a smile.

"I don't know about oxygen, but I know very well that fish die when you don't change their water. You are right. But if I assign people to constantly pump water into your cistern, it would be too expensive, more expensive than your pearls. You'll drive me bankrupt!"

Ichtiander didn't know the price of pearls or that Zurita paid his divers and sailors pennies. The young man believed him and exclaimed, "If I am unprofitable to keep, then let me go!" And Ichtiander glanced at the ocean.

"Aren't you sneaky!" Zurita laughed out loud.

"Please! I'll bring you pearls of my own free will. I have gathered a pile this high a long time ago." Ichtiander showed with his hand at knee level. "All even, smooth, each the size of a bean. I will give you all of them, just let me go."

Zurita's breath caught.

"You are lying!" Zurita said, trying to sound calm.

"I have never lied to anyone," Ichtiander became angry.

"Where is your stash?" Zurita asked, no longer concealing his excitement.

"In an underground cave. No one but Leading knows where it is."

"Leading? Who is that?"

"My dolphin."

"Indeed!"

"This is insane," Zurita thought. "If this is true – and I don't think he is lying – this surpasses anything I could have dreamed of. I will be wealthy beyond belief. The Rothchilds and Rockefellers will be paupers compared to me. I think the boy is trustworthy. Should I trust his word and let him go?"

But Zurita was a practical man. He was unaccustomed of taking anyone's word. He started thinking of better ways to lay his hands on Ichtiander's treasure. *"If only Gutierre asked Ichtiander, he wouldn't refuse to bring it to me."*

"I might let you go," Zurita said, "but you'll have to stay with me for a while. Yes. I have my own reasons. I think you won't regret this delay. In the meantime, you are my guest, albeit a reluctant one, and I want to make you comfortable. Perhaps, instead of the cistern, which would be too expensive, we could place you in a large metal cage. It would protect you from the sharks, and you can stay in the water."

"Yes, but I need to breathe regular air as well."

"Very well, we'll raise you to the deck from time to time. This would be cheaper than pumping water into the cistern. In other words, we'll set everything up to your satisfaction."

Zurita was in a great mood. He even ordered   a glass of vodka to be given to each sailor at lunch, which was unprecedented.

Ichtiander was once again taken to the hold, as the cage wasn't ready yet. With some anxiety, Zurita opened the door of his quarters and showed Gutierre his hat filled with pearls.

"I remember my promises," he said with a smile. "My wife likes pearls, and likes expensive gifts. In order to get many pearls one must have a good diver. That is why I captured Ichtiander. Look – this is one morning's catch."

Gutierre glanced briefly at the pearls. With great difficulty she suppressed an exclamation of surprise. Zurita still noticed and laughed complacently.

"You will be the wealthiest woman in Argentina, possibly in all of America. You will have everything. I shall build you a palace that will be the envy of kings. And now, to secure our truce, please accept half of these pearls."

"No! I don't want a single pearl obtained through crime," Gutierre replied abruptly. "Please, leave me alone."

Zurita was taken aback and vexed – he didn't expect such reaction.

"Only one more thing. Would you like, Madam," to sound more convincing he addressed her formally, "for me to set Ichtiander free?"

Gutierre looked at Zurita with mistrust, as if trying to guess what new trick he was playing on her.

"Yes, and then what?" she asked coldly.

"Ichtiander's fate is in your hands. All you need to do is order Ichtiander to bring to *Medusa* the pearls he keeps somewhere underwater, and I shall let the Sea Devil go anywhere he pleases."

"Remember very well what I am about to say. I do not believe a single word you say. You will get the pearls and chain Ichtiander down again. It's just as true as the fact that I am married to the most dishonest and traitorous man in the world. Remember this and don't try dragging me into your underhanded plans. Once again – please, leave me alone."

There was nothing to talk about, and Zurita left. In his own room, he transferred the pearls into a small bag, carefully put it into a trunk, locked it, and returned to the deck. The argument with his wife bothered him very little. He saw himself wealthy and surrounded by respect.

He went up to the bridge and lit a cigar. Thoughts about future wealth excited him pleasantly. Always alert, this time he did not notice the sailors talking about something in small groups.

THE ABANDONED MEDUSA

Zurita was standing by the railing across from the foremast. At the sign from the navigator, several sailors attacked Pedro at once. They weren't armed, but there were many of them. However, Zurita turned out to be a difficult adversary. Two sailors grabbed Zurita from the back. He pulled away from the group and, after a few paces, leaned back over the railing as hard as he could.

The sailors let go of their victim with a groan and fell onto the deck. Zurita straightened out and started fighting off new attackers with his fists. He was never without his revolver, but the attack was so sudden, that Zurita didn't manage to pull it from the holster. He slowly retreated to the foremast and suddenly started climbing the rigging with the agility of a monkey.

A sailor grabbed his foot, but Zurita kicked him in the head with his free foot, and the concussed sailor fell down to the deck. Zurita managed to get as high as the lower topsail and settled down there, cursing at the top of his lungs. Here he felt relatively safe. He pulled out the revolver and shouted, "The first man to come after me will get a bullet through his head!"

The sailors buzzed below, discussing what to do next.

"There are guns in the captain's quarters!" the navigator yelled, trying to out-shout everyone else. "Let's go and break down the door!"

Several sailors headed for the trapdoor.

"It's over," Zurita thought. "They'll shoot me!"

He glanced at the sea, as if looking for help. Barely able to believe his eyes, Zurita saw a submarine approaching *Medusa* with incredible speed across the smooth expanse of the ocean.

"I hope it doesn't go underwater!" Zurita thought. "There are people on the bridge. Will they notice me or pass by?"

"Help! Quickly! They are trying to kill me!" Zurita shouted at the top of his lungs.

People on the submarine must have noticed him. Maintaining the same speed, the boat kept moving straight at *Medusa*.

The armed sailors appeared from the trapdoor. They scattered around the deck and halted. An armed submarine was approaching *Medusa* – probably from the military. They couldn't very well kill Zurita before all these witnesses.

Zurita was overjoyed. But his triumph was short-lived. Balthazar and Christo were standing on the bridge of the submarine, next to a tall man with a hooked nose and eagle eyes.

The man shouted, "Pedro Zurita! You must immediately hand over the man named Ichtiander, whom you kidnapped! I am giving you five minutes, or else I'll sink your schooner."

"*Traitors!*" Zurita thought, looking at Christo and Balthazar with hatred. "*But I'd rather lose Ichtiander than my own life.*"

"Let me go get him," Zurita said, climbing down the mast. The sailors already realized they had to get out. They quickly lowered the boats or jumped into the water and swam to the shore. Each of them cared only for himself.

Zurita ran down the steps to his room, quickly grabbed the bag with pearls, stuck it into his shirt, then found some belts and a kerchief. A moment later, he unlocked Gutierre's room, snatched her up and carried her abovedeck.

"Ichtiander is unwell. You will find him belowdeck," Zurita said, still holding Gutierre. He ran to the railing, threw her in a remaining boat, lowered it, and jumped in.

The submarine couldn't pursue him now – not in shallow waters. But Gutierre saw her father on the bridge of the submarine.

"Father, save Ichtiander! He is in..." but she didn't finish, because Zurita stuffed the kerchief into her mouth, as he tightened the belts around her hands.

"Let go of the woman!" Salvator shouted as he watched this cruelty.

"This woman is my wife, and no one can interfere with my business!" Zurita shouted back, rowing hard.

"No one has the right to treat a woman like that!" Salvator shouted irritably. "Halt or I'll shoot!" But Zurita kept rowing.

Salvator took a shot. The bullet struck the side of the boat. Zurita lifted Gutierre, moved her in front of him and shouted, "Continue!"

Gutierre thrashed in his arms.

"What an exceptional scoundrel!" Salvator said and lowered his gun.

Balthazar dove off the submarine and tried to catch up with the boat. But Zurita was already close to the shore. He pushed at the oars

115

and soon the wave nudged the boat onto the sandy beach. Pedro grabbed Gutierre and vanished behind the rocks.

Once he saw that there was no catching Zurita, Balthazar swam to the schooner and climbed to the deck using the anchor chain. He went belowdeck and started looking for Ichtiander.

Balthazar went through the entire ship, all the way to the hold. But there was no one there.

"Ichtiander is not on the schooner!" Balthazar shouted to Salvator.

"But he is alive and must be somewhere nearby! Gutierre said, 'Ichtiander is in...' Had this rascal not covered her mouth, we would have known where to look for him," Christo said.

Looking at the surface of the sea, Christo noticed tips of masts sticking from the water.

A ship must have sunk here recently. Could Ichtiander be there?

"What if Zurita sent Ichtiander to look for treasure on that sunken ship?" Christo said.

Balthazar picked up the chain with a circle on one end.

"Zurita must have lowered Ichtiander down on this chain. Ichtiander would have gotten away otherwise. No, he can't be on the sunken ship."

"Yes," Salvator said thoughtfully. "We scared away Zurita but haven't found Ichtiander."

THE SHIPWRECK

Zurita's pursuers didn't know about the events that took place on *Medusa* that morning.

The sailors spent all night conspiring and made a decision by morning – to attack Zurita at the first opportunity, kill him, and take control of Ichtiander and the schooner.

Early in the morning, Zurita came out to the bridge. All was still, and Medusa was moving slowly, doing no more than three knots per hour.

Zurita was peering at something out in the ocean. Through his binoculars he recognized the radio antennae of a sunken ship.

Soon, Zurita noticed a lifesaver floating in the water.

Zurita ordered to lower the boat and get the lifesaver.

When they brought it back to the ship, Zurita read the inscription *Mafaldou*.

"*Mafaldou* went under?" Zurita was surprised. He knew all about that large American post and passenger steamship. Such a ship would contain many valuables. "*Could Ichtiander get these things off the ship? Is the chain long enough? Unlikely. And if I send Ichtiander without the chain, he won't come back.*"

Zurita thought about it. His greed wrestled with his fear of losing Ichtiander.

Medusa slowly approached the masts poking out of the water.

The sailors crowded on one side. The wind faded entirely. *Medusa* halted.

I served on *Mafaldou* once," one of the sailors said. "A nice big ship. An entire floating city. And the passengers were all rich Americans."

"Mafaldou went under but apparently had no chance to send a radiogram about its emergency," Zurita pondered. "Perhaps, their radio was damaged. Otherwise every launch, speed-boat, and yacht would have rushed to it, carrying government representatives, journalists, photographers, cameramen, and scuba divers. I can't delay. I'll have to risk letting Ichtiander go without the chain. There is no other way. But how can I force him to come back? And if I do have to take this risk, wouldn't it be better to send Ichtiander for his pearl stash. But is the stash really that valuable? Or is Ichtiander exaggerating?"

Of course, he could try and get both the pearls and the treasure buried on *Mafaldou*. The pearls weren't going anywhere, no one could find them without Ichtiander, as long as Ichtiander himself remained under Zurita's control. But in a few days, or perhaps a few hours, *Mafaldou*'s riches might be gone.

"*Well then, Mafaldou first*," Zurita decided. He ordered to drop the anchor. He then went to his room, wrote something on a piece of paper and took it to Ichtiander's room.

"Can you read, Ichtiander? Gutierre sent you a note."

Ichtiander quickly took the note and read, "Ichtiander! Please do this for me. There is a shipwreck next to *Medusa*. Go there and bring back everything valuable you can find. Zurita will let you go without a chain, but you must return to *Medusa*. Do this for me, Ichtiander, and soon you shall be free. Gutierre."

Ichtiander never received a letter from Gutierre and did not know her handwriting. He was very glad to receive the letter, but also wondered about it. What if it was another one of Zurita's tricks?

"Why didn't Gutierre ask me herself?" Ichtiander asked, pointing at the note.

"She is not feeling well," Zurita replied, "but you shall see her as soon as you return."

"Why does Gutierre want these things?" Ichtiander asked mistrustfully.

"If you were a real man, you wouldn't be asking such questions. What woman doesn't want to dress well and wear expensive jewelry? In order to do that, one must have money. There is a lot of money at the shipwreck. It doesn't belong to anyone now, so why not get it for Gutierre? The main thing is to find gold coins. There should be some leather bags in the postal hold. In addition, gold jewelry and gems worn by passengers."

"Do you really think I would search dead bodies?" Ichtiander asked indignantly. "I don't believe you. Gutierre is not greedy, and she would never send me to do such a thing.

"Damn it!" Zurita exclaimed. He saw that his plan was about to fall apart if he failed to convince Ichtiander.

Zurita recovered, laughed good-naturedly and said, "I see you won't be deceived. I'll have to be honest with you. Listen. Gutierre is not the one who wants to have the gold from *Mafaldou* – it's me. Do you believe that?"

Ichtiander smiled despite himself, "Absolutely!"

"Excellent! You are beginning to trust me – which means we can make a deal. Yes, I need the gold. And if there is enough of it on *Mafaldou* to compare to your pearl stash, I will immediately let you go into the ocean, as soon as you bring me the gold. But here is the trouble – you don't entirely trust me, and I don't entirely trust you. I am afraid that if I let you out without the chain, you will dive in and…"

"If I give you my word to return, I shall keep it."

"I had no chance to verify that. You don't like me, and I won't be surprised if you don't keep your word. But you love Gutierre, and you will do as she asks you. Right? And so I made a deal with her. Of course, she wants me to set you free. That is why she wrote a letter and gave it to me, wanting to help you get your freedom. Do you understand?"

Everything Zurita said seemed convincing and plausible to Ichtiander. Ichtiander didn't realize that Zurita promised to set him free only when he was convinced that the value of gold from *Mafaldou* equaled that of his pearls.

"In order to compare the two," Zurita thought to himself, "Ichtiander would have to bring his pearls – I shall demand it. And then I'll have Mafaldou's gold, the pearl stash, and Ichtiander."

But Ichtiander could not have known what Zurita was thinking. Zurita's sincerity convinced him, and Ichtiander agreed.

Zurita let out the sigh of relief.

"He won't trick me," he thought.

"Come quickly."

Ichtiander swiftly went abovedeck and dove into the sea.

The sailors saw him diving without the chain. They understood immediately that Ichtiander was going after *Mafaldou*'s treasures. Was Zurita going to get all of the riches yet again? They could delay no longer and attacked Zurita.

As the crew went after Zurita, Ichtiander explored the shipwreck.

Through the huge trapdoor in the upper deck, the young man swam down following the stairs resembling a grand staircase of a large house. He found himself in a large corridor.

It was almost dark. Some weak light fell through the open doors.

Ichtiander went through one of the doorways and entered the salon. Large round portholes shed faint light over the huge hall that could house several hundred people. Ichtiander settled onto a gorgeous chandelier and looked around. It was a strange sight. Wooden chairs and small tables floated up and rocked by the ceiling. There was a small stage with a grand piano. Soft carpets covered the floor. The lacquered redwood wainscoting on the walls became warped here and there. There were potted palm trees arranged by one of the walls.

Ichtiander pushed away from the chandelier and floated toward the palms. Suddenly, he halted in astonishment. Some man was swimming toward him, repeating all his movements. "A mirror," Ichtiander realized. The enormous mirror took up the entire wall, dully reflecting the salon's furnishings.

There was no point in looking for treasure here. Ichtiander returned to the corridor, descended one deck, and swam into another space, as luxurious and large as the salon – most likely, a restaurant. On the bar shelves and racks, there were bottles of wine, cans of sardines and boxes. The pressure drove many corks into the bottles and warped some of the cans. Some of the settings remained on the table, but some of the dishes, silver forks and knives fell to the floor.

Ichtiander made his way to the passengers' quarters.

He visited several rooms furnished according to the latest standard of American comfort, but didn't find a single corpse. Only one room had a water-logged corpse floating by the ceiling.

"Many of them must have escaped in the boats," Ichtiander thought.

When he went one deck lower, where third-class passengers traveled, the young man saw a terrible scene – the rooms were filled with men, women, and children. The corpses included white people, Chinese, Negroes, and Indians.

The ship's crew must have rushed to save the wealthy first-class passengers, leaving the rest to fend for themselves. Ichtiander could not even get into some of the rooms as the doors were stacked high with corpses.

In all the panic, people had trampled teach other, filled the doorways, getting in each other's way and depriving themselves of the escape.

Corpses floated slowly in the long hallway.

Water had rushed in through the open portholes and now carried the swollen bodies. Ichtiander became frightened and rushed to leave this underwater cemetery.

"Didn't Gutierre know where she was sending me?" Ichtiander wondered. Could she really have made him turn out the drowned people's pockets and open their suitcases? No, she couldn't have done that! Apparently, he once again fell for one of Zurita's lies. *"I shall go to the surface,"* Ichtiander decided, *"and demand for Gutierre to come out and confirm her request."*

The young man glided along the endless passages from one deck to the next like a fish and swiftly reached the surface. He approached *Medusa*.

"Zurita!" he called. "Gutierre!"

But no one answered. *Medusa* silently rocked upon the waves.

"Where did they all go?" the young man thought. *"Is Zurita planning something again?"* Ichtiander carefully swam up to the schooner and climbed on deck.

"Gutierre!" he called again.

"We are here!" he heard Zurita's voice, barely audible from the shore.

Ichtiander turned and saw Zurita peeking out from behind the shrubs on the shore.

"Gutierre is sick! Swim here, Ichtiander!" Zurita shouted. Gutierre was ill! He would see her. Ichtiander jumped into the water and quickly headed to the shore.

He only just emerged from the water, when he heard Gutierre's muffled voice, "Zurita is lying! Run, Ichtiander!"

The boy quickly turned and swam away underwater. When he got far enough from the shore, he surfaced and glanced back. He saw a flash of something white on the shore.

Perhaps, it was Gutierre congratulating him on his escape. Would he ever see her again?

Ichtiander quickly headed into the open ocean. There was a small ship in the distance. Surrounded by foam, the ship headed to the south, slicing through the water with its sharp bow.

"I should get away from people," Ichtiander thought, dove deep down and vanished underwater.

PART THREE

THE NEW-FOUND FATHER

After the unsuccessful submarine trip, Balthazar was in the worst of moods. They didn't find Ichtiander, and Zurita disappeared along with Gutierre.

"Those damn whites!" the old man grumbled, as he sat alone at his shop. "They chased us off our land and turned us into slaves. They cripple our children and kidnap our daughters. They want to exterminate all of us to the last person."

"Hello brother!" Balthazar heard Christo's voice. "I've got news! Big news! Ichtiander turned up."

"What?!" Balthazar rose quickly. "Tell me quickly!"

"I will, just don't interrupt me, or I'll forget what I was trying to say. Ichtiander turned up. I was right that time – he was at the shipwreck. We sailed away, and he surfaced and went home."

"Where is he? At Salvator's?"

"Yes, at Salvator's."

"I am going to him, to Salvator and will demand to give me back my son."

"He won't!" Christo objected. "Salvator is not letting Ichtiander swim in the ocean. I let him out in secret now and then."

"He will! If he doesn't, then I'll kill Salvator. Let's go now." Christo waved him off in fright.

"At least wait until tomorrow. I barely got permission from Salvator to visit my 'granddaughter'. Salvator has become so suspicious. Every time he looks into my eyes, it's like he is stabbing me with a knife. I am begging you, wait until tomorrow."

"Fine. I'll go to Salvator tomorrow. And now I'll go over there, to the bay. Maybe I'll see my son from the distance."

Balthazar sat on the rocks by the bay all night, peering into the wave. The seas were stormy. Cold southern winds blew in gusts, tearing the foam off the tops of the waves and scattering it over the shore side cliffs. Surf thundered on the beach. The moon, diving in and out of the clouds rushing across the sky sometimes lit up the waves, and sometimes vanished. As hard as Balthazar tried, he could not see anything in the stormy ocean. The dawn came, and Balthazar was still sitting motionless on the rocks. The ocean turned from dark to gray, but it was still deserted and lifeless.

Suddenly Balthazar looked up, startled. His keen eyes noticed a dark object floating in the waves. It was a man! What if he was drowning? But no, he was resting calmly on his back, with his arms folding behind his head. Was it him?

Balthazar was right. It was Ichtiander. Balthazar rose, and clasping his hands to his chest, shouted, "Ichtiander! My son!" The old man raised his arms and dove into the sea. Having dropped off the cliff, he dove deep down. But when he surfaced, there was no one around. Struggling with the waves Balthazar dove again, but a huge wave caught him, flipped him over, threw him on the shore, and rolled away with dull rumbling.

Soaking wet, Balthazar rose, looked back at the waves and sighed heavily. "Did I imagine it?"

When wind and sun dried Balthazar's clothes, he went to the wall protecting Salvator's property and knocked on the metal gate.

"Who is there?" the Negro servant asked, peeking through the peephole.

"I am here to see the doctor about an important matter."

"The doctor is not seeing anyone," the Negro replied and shut the peephole.

Balthazar continued knocking and shouting but nobody opened. All he could hear beyond the gates was the menacing barking of dogs.

"Just you wait, damned Spaniard!" Balthazar shook his fist at the gates and went to the city.

Not far from the court building there was a pub called *The Palm Tree* – an old, squat, white building with thick stone walls. There was a small verandah in front of the entrance with a striped canvas awning protecting it from the sun, and cacti in blue enameled pots. The verandah came to life only in the evenings. During the day, the customers preferred to sit in the cool low-ceiling rooms. In a way, the pub was like a department of the courthouse. Plaintiffs, defendants, witnesses, and the accused yet to be arrested came here during the court sessions.

They preferred spending the boring hours waiting their turn here, drinking beer and palm wine. A quick-footed boy constantly running back and forth between the courthouse and *The Palm Tree* told them about everything that was going on in the courtroom. This was convenient.

Lawyers of questionable repute and false witnesses came here too, openly offering their services.

Balthazar has been at *The Palm Tree* many times regarding his shop. He knew this was the right place to find someone to write up an appeal. This was why Balthazar came here.

He quickly crossed the verandah, entered the cool vestibule, indulgently breathed the cool air, wiped the sweat off his forehead and asked a boy who ran up to him, "Is Larra here?"

"Don Flores de Larra is here, in his usual place," the boy rattled off.

The man by the grand name of Don Flores de Larra once was a small court clerk. He was fired for bribery. Presently, he had many clients – those who engaged in questionable activities happily appealed to this great quibbler. Balthazar had business with him too.

Larra was sitting by the gothic window with a wide sill. On the table before the solicitor sat a mug of wine and a fat rust-colored briefcase. His ever-ready fountain pen was clipped to the pocket of his worn olive-colored suit.

Larra was fat, bald, ruddy, red-nosed, clean-shaven, and proud. The breeze fluttering in through the window ruffled what was left of his fringe of grey hair. The judge himself could not have received his clients with greater imperiousness.

Noticing Balthazar, he nodded carelessly, gestured him to a wicker chair across the table and said, "Sit down, please. What have you got for me? Would you like some beer? Palm wine?"

He ordered, but the client was usually the one who paid. Balthazar didn't seem to hear.

"A big case. An important case, Larra."

"Don Flores de Larra," the solicitor corrected, sipping from his mug. Balthazar paid no attention to the correction.

"What is the nature of your case?"

"You know, Larra…"

"Don Flores de…"

"Leave this nonsense for the newbies!" Balthazar shouted angrily. "This is a serious matter."

"Then tell me about it," Larra replied in a different tone of voice.

"Do you know the Sea Devil?"

"I don't have the honor of knowing him personally, but I have heard much about him," Larra replied with his usual pompousness.

"Right! The man known as the Sea Devil is my son Ichtiander."

"Impossible!" Larra exclaimed. "You must have had too much to drink, Balthazar."

The Indian slammed the table with his fist, "I haven't had anything in my mouth since yesterday, save for a few mouthfuls of sea water."

"Then it's even worse."

"Are you saying I'm mad? No, I am in complete possession of my wits. Be quiet and listen." Balthazar told Larra the entire story. Larra listened to the Indian without speaking a single word. His grey eyebrows rose higher and higher. Finally, he couldn't stand it, forgot his Olympian grandeur, slapped the table with his fat hand and shouted, "A million devils!"

A boy in a white apron and with a dirty napkin ran up.

"What would you like?"

"Two bottles of Sauterne with ice!" Turning to Balthazar, Larra said, "Splendid! A beautiful case! Did you think all this up by yourself? Although, I must admit, your fatherhood is the weakest link in all this."

"Do you question me?" Balthazar turned red with anger.

"Come, come, don't be mad, old chap. I am speaking as a lawyer, from the standpoint of the plausibility of legal proof — it is somewhat weak. But we can fix that. Yes. And make a lot of money."

"I need my son, not the money," Balthazar objected.

"Everyone needs money, especially those who expect their family to expand, as you do," Larra said sanctimoniously and continued, squinting mischievously, "The most valuable and reliable thing in this entire case is that we have found out what sort of experiments and surgeries Salvator performs. We could set up a minefield to get this moneybag Salvator to start spilling pesetas like overripe oranges in a storm."

Balthazar barely touched the glass of wine poured by Larra and said, "I want to get back my son. You must write a statement about it for the court."

"No-no! Absolutely not!" Larra objected, almost with a fright. "Starting with this would ruin the entire case. We should save this for the end."

"Then what do you advise?" Balthazar asked.

"First," Larra ticked off one fat finger, "we shall send Salvator a letter, composed in the most sophisticated language. We shall inform him that we know all about his unlawful surgeries and experiments. If he wants us to keep from making the matter public, he must pay us a round sum. A hundred thousand. Yes, a hundred thousand at the very least." Larra paused and gave Balthazar a questioning look.

The latter frowned and remained silent.

"Second," Larra continued. "When we receive the requested sum – and we will receive it – we shall send Professor Salvator another letter, composed with even more sophistication. We shall tell him that we have found Ichtiander's real father and have unquestionable proof. We will write to him that the father desires to get his son back and will not hesitate to file a lawsuit, during which it might become known that Salvator has disfigured Ichtiander. If Salvator wants to avoid the lawsuit and keep the boy, he should pay a million dollars to the people we send to a specific place at a specific time."

But Balthazar was not listening. He grabbed the bottle and was preparing to throw it at the solicitor's head. Larra had never seen Balthazar so enraged.

"Don't be mad. Leave it, I was kidding. Put down the bottle!" Larra exclaimed, covering his glossy skull with his hand.

"You! You!" Balthazar shouted, beside himself. "You are offering me to sell my own son, to give up Ichtiander. Have you no heart? Or are you not a person, but a scorpion, a tarantula? Don't you know anything of fatherly love?"

"Five! Five! Five!" Larra shouted back, also becoming angry. "Five times over! I have five sons! Five little demons of every size! Five mouths to feed! I know, I understand, I feel! You'll get yours, don't worry. Be patient and listen."

Balthazar calmed down. He returned the bottle to the table, lowered his head and glanced at Larra, "Well, come on!"

"There you go! Salvator will pay us a million. This will be your Ichtiander's estate. I'll get a bit from it too. For the trouble and for the authorship – a mere hundred thousand. We'll agree on something. Salvator will pay a million, I swear! As soon as he does…"

"We sue him."

"A little more patience. We will offer the publishers and editors of the largest news company to pay us, say, twenty or thirty thousand – for minor expenses – for our information about a sensational crime. Perhaps we'll manage to get something from the funds set aside for the secret police. After all, detectives can build a career on a case like that. When we squeeze out of Salvator everything possible, then you'll be free to go to court and declare your fatherly love, and may Nemesis herself help you prove your rights and receive your beloved son into your loving embrace." Larra downed a glass of wine, slammed the empty glass on the table, and looked at Balthazar triumphantly.

"What do you think?"

"I can't eat or sleep. And you suggest that we drag this out," Balthazar began.

"But why?" Larra interrupted him heatedly. "What for? For the sake of millions. Millions! Don't you understand? You managed to live twenty years without Ichtiander."

"I did. And now... In other words, write up the statement for the court."

"You really are not thinking clearly!" Larra exclaimed. "Come to your senses, wake up, be sensible, Balthazar! Understand! Millions! Money! Gold! We can buy anything we want. The best tobacco, a car, twenty boats, this pub."

"Write the statement, or I shall go to another solicitor," Balthazar stated firmly.

Larra realized there was no use arguing anymore. He shook his head, sighed, pulled out paper from his briefcase and the fountain pen from his pocket.

In a few minutes the complaint that Salvator has unlawfully kidnapped and disfigured Balthazar's son was complete.

"I am telling you one last time – be sensible," Larra said.

"Give it here," the Indian said, reaching for the paper.

"Submit it to the chief prosecutor. Do you know him?" Larra instructed his client and mumbled under his breath, "I hope you fall off the stairs and break a leg."

When he left the prosecutor's office and was walking down the large white staircase, Balthazar ran into Zurita.

"What are you doing here?" Zurita asked looking at the Indian suspiciously. "Are you complaining about me?"

"I could complain about all of you," Balthazar replied meaning all Spaniards, "but there is no one to complain to. Where are you keeping my daughter?"

"How dare you talk to me like that?" Zurita turned red. "If you weren't my wife's father, I would have beaten you with a stick."

Zurita rudely shoved Balthazar aside, walked up the steps and vanished behind the large oak door.

A JUDICIAL CONUNDRUM

The Chief Prosecutor of Buenos Aires received a visit from a rare guest – the priest from the local cathedral Bishop Juan de Garsilasso.

The prosecutor, a short, fat, very lively man with small eyes, short hair, and pomaded mustache, rose from his seat to greet the bishop.

The host welcomed the honored guest to a heavy leather armchair by the desk.

The bishop and the prosecutor looked nothing like each other. The prosecutor's face was fleshy and red, with thick lips and wide, pear-like nose. His fingers looked like fat short sausages, and the buttons over his round belly looked ready to pop at any moment, unable to contain the wobbling might of his girth.

The bishop's face was striking in its thinness and pallor. His thin aquiline nose, sharp chin, and thin, almost bluish lips, made him look like a stereotypical Jesuit.

The bishop never looked his companion straight in the eye, but nevertheless he was watching everything very carefully. The bishop's influence was tremendous, and he happily stepped away from church matters to engage in complex political games.

Having greeted his host, the bishop immediately proceeded to the purpose of his visit.

"I would like to know," the bishop said quietly, "the state of affairs with Professor Salvator's case."

"Ah, so you too are interested in this matter, Your Eminence!" the prosecutor exclaimed pleasantly. "Yes, it is an exceptional case!" Picking up a heavy folder from his desk and leafing through the pages of the case, the prosecutor continued, "Based on Pedro Zurita's claim, we conducted a search at Professor Salvator's residence. Zurita's statement that Salvator conducted unusual surgeries with animals was fully confirmed. Salvator's gardens were a veritable factory of monstrous creatures. It's astonishing! For example, Salvator..."

"I know about the results of the search from the papers," the bishop interrupted gently. "What measures have you taken regarding Salvator himself? Was he arrested?"

"Yes, he was. In addition, we have transferred to the city the young man named Ichtiander, both as material proof and a witness for the prosecution. He is also known as the Sea Devil. Who could have thought, that the famous Sea Devil who occupied us for so long would end up being one of the monsters from Salvator's zoo! Presently, the experts, the university professors, are engaged in studying all these monsters. Of course, we could not transport the entire zoo, all these pieces of living proof, to the city. But Ichtiander has been brought in and settled in the court building basement. He has been causing us many issues. Imagine, we had to build him a large cistern, as he cannot live without water. Indeed, he was very ill at first. Apparently, Salvator has made some unusual changes in his body, having turned the boy into the amphibian man. Our scientists are working on this question."

"I am more interested in the fate of Salvator," the bishop said as quietly as before. "According to which article of law is he being held responsible? And what is your opinion – will he be found guilty?"

"Salvator's case is a rare legal puzzle," the prosecutor replied. "I admit, I haven't decided yet how to classify this crime. The simplest thing, of course, would be to accuse Salvator of conducting illegal vivisections and the injury he inflicted on the boy."

The bishop started frowning, "Do you suppose that all these actions do not amount to a crime?"

"They do, but how much of a crime do they amount to?" the prosecutor continued. "I received another statement – from some Indian named Balthazar. He says that Ichtiander is his son. His proof is a little weak, but we could use the Indian as a witness for the prosecution, if the experts establish that Ichtiander really is his son."

"Then, in the best possible case, Salvator will be accused only of violating laws of medicine and will only be tried for conducting a surgery on a child without permission of his parents?"

"And possibly for inflicting injury on the child. That is more serious. But there is one complication in this case. The experts – although this is not their final conclusion – believe that a normal person could not have thought of experimenting with animals like that and conducting such unusual surgeries. Salvator could be declared incompetent due to mental illness."

The bishop sat silently, gazing at the corner of the desk, his thin lips pursed. He then said very quietly, "I didn't expect this from you."

"Didn't expect what, Your Eminence?" the puzzled prosecutor asked.

"Even you, the sentinel of justice, seem to justify Salvator's actions by stating that his surgeries had some reason behind them."

"What is so bad about it?"

"You are having difficulty identifying his crime. The judgment of the church – and that of heaven – sees Salvator's actions differently. Allow me to come to your aid and offer you some advice."

"Please," the prosecutor said, taken aback. The bishop started speaking in a low voice, gradually raising it, like a preacher or an accuser, "You say that there is some sense to Salvator's actions. You believe that the disfigured animals and the boy might have received some benefits in the process, which they did not have before? What does it mean? Did the Creator make people imperfectly? Was Professor Salvator's interference necessary to improve on His creation?"

The prosecutor remained still, looking down.

He found himself the accused before the church. He did not expect this.

"Have you forgotten what is said in the Holy Writ, in the Book of Genesis, chapter one, verse twenty-six, 'And God said – I shall create man in my image,' followed by verse twenty-seven, 'And God created man in His image'. Salvator dared to distort that image and likeness, and you – even you! – find it justifiable!"

"Forgive me, Holy Father," the prosecutor said.

"Didn't the Lord find his creation beautiful," the bishop said with conviction, "and complete? You remember the articles of human law very well, but forget those of God's law. Remember verse thirty-one of the same chapter of the Book of Genesis, 'And God saw all that He created and said it was good.' Your Salvator believes that something must be corrected, redone, disfigured, that people ought to be amphibian creatures – and you find this reasonable and even clever. Is this not an insult to God? Is this not sacrilege? Is this not an atrocity? Or do our secular laws no longer punish religious crimes? What happens, if others follow you and start saying, 'Yes, man was made imperfectly by God. We should give man over to Doctor Salvator for improvements.'? Is this not a monstrous undermining of religion? God found all that he made good – all of His creations. Salvator is switching animals' heads, changes their skins, creates truly revolting monsters, as if mocking the Creator. And after all this, you are having trouble finding a crime to accuse Salvator of!"

The bishop paused. He was pleased with the impression his speech had on the prosecutor. Then, he once again started speaking quietly, gradually raising his voice, "I said I was more interested in Salvator's fate. But how can I be indifferent to Ichtiander's fate as well? After all, this creature doesn't even have a Christian name, for Ichtiander means man-fish in Greek. Even if Ichtiander himself is not guilty of anything, even if he is nothing but a victim, he is still a godless atrocious creature. His very existence can confuse people, lead them to sinful thoughts, tempt the young and unsettle those weak in their faith. Ichtiander must not exist! It would be best if God called upon him, if this unfortunate boy died of the imperfections in his disfigured nature," the bishop gave the prosecutor a meaningful look. "In any case, he must be accused, taken out of society, and deprived of his freedom. After all, he too committed a few crimes – stole fish from the fishermen, cut their nets and, finally, frightened them to the extent that they stopped working, leaving the city without fish. The godless Salvator and his disgusting creation Ichtiander represent a daring challenge to the church, God, and heaven! The church shall not lay down its arms, until they are eliminated."

The bishop continued his accusations. The prosecutor sat before him, crushed and slumped, not even attempting to interrupt this flow of menacing words.

When the bishop finished, the prosecutor rose, walked up to him and said in a subdued voice, "As a Christian, I shall take my sin to confession, to be absolved. As a government official, I thank you for the assistance you provided. Salvator's crime is now clear to me. He shall be charged and punished accordingly. The sword of justice will not spare Ichtiander either."

THE GENIUS MADMAN

The trial failed to break Doctor Salvator. While in prison, he remained calm and self-assured and spoke to the investigators and experts with haughty condescension, like a grownup talking to children.

He couldn't stand inaction. He wrote a lot and conducted several brilliant surgeries in prison. His patients included the wife of the prison warden. A malignant tumor threatened her life. Salvator saved her at the very moment when other physicians refused to help, stating that medicine was helpless in her case.

The trial day finally came.

The enormous courtroom was not large enough to house everyone wishing to watch the proceedings.

The public crowded the corridors, filled the square in front of the building, and peeked through the open windows. Many of the curious climbed the trees growing around the court building.

Salvator calmly took his place. He acted with such dignity that one would think he was the judge and not the accused. Salvator declined services of an attorney.

Hundreds of eyes were watching him. But only a few could stand Salvator's searching gaze.

Ichtiander inspired equal amounts of interest, but he was not in the courtroom. In the last few days, Ichtiander felt poorly and spent almost all of his time in the water cistern, hiding from the annoyingly curious. In Salvator's case, Ichtiander was merely a witness for the prosecution, or rather, a piece of material proof, as the prosecutor called him.

Ichtiander's case regarding his criminal activities was to be heard separately, after Salvator's trial.

The prosecutor had to follow this course of action, because the bishop was impatient about Salvator's case, while gathering evidence against Ichtiander would have required time. The prosecutor's agents actively, although cautiously, hired witnesses for the future trial, in which Ichtiander would be the main defendant, at the pub *The Palm Tree*. The bishop, however, continued to hint to the prosecutor, that the best outcome would be if God took away the ill-fated Ichtiander. Such death would be the best proof that man could only damage God's creatures and not improve them.

Three science experts from the university presented their summary.

The audience listened to the scientists' opinions with great attention, trying not to miss a single word.

"Following the request of this court," the middle-aged Professor Shayne, the chief scientific expert, began, "we examined the animals and the young man Ichtiander, subject to the surgeries conducted by Professor Salvator at his laboratory. We have also examined his small, bit skillfully equipped laboratories and operation rooms. In his operations, Professor Salvator not only used the latest improvements in surgical technology, such as electric scalpels, disinfecting ultraviolet light and such, but also tools that are not yet known to modern surgeons. Apparently, they were manufactured according to his instructions. I won't spend much time on Professor Salvator's experiments with animals. The essence of these experiments is in a series of operations, exceptionally daring in their conception and brilliant in their execution – transplants of tissues and entire organs, connecting two animals, turning amphibians into single-environment creatures and vice versa, turning females into males, and discovering new methods of slowing down the aging process. In Salvator's gardens we found children of fourteen years old and younger, belonging to various Indian tribes."

"What was the condition of the children?" the prosecutor asked.

"The children were all healthy and happy. They were playing in the garden and enjoying themselves. Many of them were delivered by Salvator from certain death. The Indians trusted him greatly and brought their children from most faraway places – from Alaska to Terra del Fuego: Eskimos, Jagans, Apaches, Taulipangs, Sanapans, Botokudes, Panos, and Araucas."

Someone in the audience gasped.

"Every tribe took their children to Salvator".

The prosecutor was becoming anxious. After his conversation with the bishop, just as his thoughts took new direction, he could not listen calmly to these praised to Salvator. He asked the expert, "Do you believe that Salvator's surgeries were useful and sensible?"

The judge, a grizzled man with a stern face, afraid that the expert might give an affirmative answer, quickly interrupted, "The court is not

134

interested in the expert's personal opinion regarding scientific subjects. Please continue. What were the results of examining the young Arauca man Ichtiander?"

"He wore a suit of artificial scales over his entire body," the expert continued, "made of some unknown substance that is flexible and extremely strong. The analysis of this substance is not yet complete. In the water, Ichtiander sometimes used glasses with special lenses made of heavy flint glass, with refraction index of almost two. This gave him the ability to see well underwater. When we took the scale suit off, we discovered round openings under his shoulder blades, each about four inches in diameter, covered with five thin strips, similar to a shark's gills."

A subdued exclamation of surprise sounded from the audience.

"Yes," the expert continued, "this appears impossible, but Ichtiander has both human lungs and a shark's gills. That is why he can exist both on land and underwater."

"The amphibian man?" the prosecutor asked sarcastically.

"Yes, in a sense, he is the amphibian man – a creature with two breathing systems."

"But how did Ichtiander come to possess a shark's gills?" the judge asked.

The expert spread his hands and replied, "That is a puzzle, which Professor Salvator will, perhaps, explain to us. Our opinion was as follows – according to Haeckel's postulate, every living creature in its development repeats all the forms that its species has been through in the course of its existence on Earth. We can state confidently that humans originated from ancestors who once used to have gills."

The prosecutor rose in his seat, but the judge gestured him to remain silent.

"On the twentieth day of human embryo's development, it has four gill folds. But later, the gills transform – the first fold turns into the auditory canal with the appropriate bone structure; the lower edge of the same fold turns into the lower jaw; the second fold turns into the hyoid bone; the third – into the throat cartilage. We don't think that Professor Salvator managed to slow down Ichtiander's development as an embryo. Although, there have been cases when fully grown individuals had a gill opening on the neck, under the jaw. It is known as the neck fistula. But, of course, one cannot live underwater with such rudimentary gills. If the embryo's development was abnormal, two things would happen – the gills would have fully developed, but at the cost of the hearing apparatus and other anatomic abnormalities. But then, Ichtiander would have turned into a monster with an underdeveloped head of a half-fish/half-man. Otherwise, the normal development would have prevailed, but at the cost of the vanishing gills.

"However, Ichtiander is a normal young man with good hearing, fully developed lower jaw, and normal lungs. In addition, he has fully formed gills. We do not know how exactly the lungs and the gills function, how they interact with each other, and whether the water passes through the mouth and lungs into the gills or penetrates directly into the gills through a small opening we discovered on Ichtiander's body just above the round gill opening. We could only answer these questions by performing an autopsy. Once again, this is a question to be answered by Professor Salvator himself. He must explain to us, how the dogs that look like jaguars came about, the amphibian monkeys, other strange unusual animals, and Ichtiander himself."

"What is your overall conclusion?" the judge asked the expert.

Professor Shayne, who himself was a well-known scientist and surgeon, replied honestly, "I admit, I don't understand much in this case. I can only say that what Professor Salvator did could only be managed by a genius. Salvator must have decided that in his skill, as a surgeon, he had reached the level, at which he could disassemble, reassemble, and adjust an animal or a human body according to his wishes. While his realization was brilliant, the daring and the breadth of his ideas are borderline... insane."

Salvator chuckled disdainfully.

He didn't know that the experts decided to lighten his sentence by raising the question of his sanity, to make it possible to replace a prison sentence by a commitment to a mental institution.

"I am not stating that he is mad," the expert continued, noticing Salvator's chuckle," but, in any case, we believe that the accused must be placed in a mental clinic and subject to a long-term observation by psychiatrists."

"The court has not considered the question of the defendant's sanity. The court shall discuss this new circumstance," the judge said. "Professor Salvator, do you wish to provide explanation to some of the questions raised by the experts and the prosecutor?"

"Yes," Salvator replied. "I shall provide explanations. May this also be considered my closing statement."

THE DEFENDANT'S STATEMENT

Salvator rose calmly and surveyed the court room as if looking for someone. In the audience, Salvator noticed Balthazar, Christo, and Zurita. The bishop was sitting in the front row. Salvator rested his gaze on him for a while. A barely noticeable smile appeared on his face. Then Salvator once again surveyed the room, looking carefully at every row.

"I am not seeing the victim in this room," Salvator finally said.

"I am the victim!" Balthazar suddenly shouted and jumped from his seat. Christo pulled his brothers sleeve and forced him to sit down.

"What victim are you talking about?" the judge asked. "If you mean the animals you disfigured, the court did not consider it necessary to demonstrate them here. But Ichtiander, the amphibian man, is in the court building."

"I mean God," Salvator replied calmly and seriously.

Having heard this answer, the judge leaned back in his chair in confusion, "Did Salvator go mad? Or is he trying to pretend to be mad to avoid prison?"

"What are you trying to say?" the judge asked.

"I believe the court should find it very clear," Salvator replied. "Who is the main and sole victim in this case? Apparently, only God. His authority, according to this court, has been undermined by my actions, by my interfering in His field. He was happy with his creations, and suddenly some doctor showed up and said, 'This is poorly made. This needs to be redone.' And started remaking God's creatures in his own way."

"This is sacrilege! I demand to include the defendant's words into the protocol," the prosecutor said with the air of a man insulted in his most sacred feelings.

Salvator shrugged his shoulders, "I am only summarizing the essence of the accusations against me. Isn't this the gist? I have read the case. Initially, I was accused of conducting vivisections and causing injury. Now I am also accused of sacrilege. Where did that come from? Perhaps, from the direction of the cathedral?"

Professor Salvator looked at the bishop.

"You yourself have created a case, in which God is the victim, and Charles Darwin and I are the defendants. I realize I might offend those in the audience by what I have to say, but I insist that the organisms of animals and humans are not perfect and require improvement. I hope that

Bishop Juan de Garsilasso, who is the prior of the cathedral and is present here, will confirm as much."

These words caused a sense of astonishment in the audience.

"In nineteen fifteen, shortly before my departure to the front," Salvator continued, "I had to make a small correction in the organism of the honorable bishop. Namely, I removed his appendix, this useless and harmful cecal appendage. As he rested on the operating table my devoutly religious patient, as I recall, had no objection to the perversion of God's image I was performing with my scalpel by cutting away a part of the bishop's body. Isn't that right?" Salvator asked, leveling his gaze at the bishop.

Juan de Garsilasso remained still. Only his pale cheeks turned slightly pink and his thin fingers started shaking.

"And wasn't there another case, when I still had a private practice and was working on the problem of slowing down aging? Didn't I receive an appeal for rejuvenation from the respected Chief Prosecutor Augusto de..."

The prosecutor wanted to object, but his words were drowned out by the laughter from the audience.

"Please stay on topic," the judge said sternly.

"This request would be much more appropriate in reference to the court itself," Salvator replied. "It wasn't me, but the court that presented the topic as it did. Wasn't anyone here scared by the thought that everyone present here is nothing but a recent monkey or even a fish, who received ability to speak and hear, because its gill folds transformed into the organs of speech and hearing? Or, if not a monkey or a fish, then its direct descendant." Addressing the prosecutor who was showing signs of impatience, Salvator said, "Calm down! I have no intention of arguing or lecturing anyone in Theory of Evolution."

After a pause, Salvator said, "The trouble is not that man originated from animals, but that he never stopped being an animal. A coarse, mean, senseless animal. My colleague need not have frightened you. There was no need to mention the development of an embryo. I did not interfere with an embryo and did not use hybridization. I am a surgeon. The scalpel was my only tool. As a surgeon, I had to help many people, I had to treat them. As I operated on patients, I often had to transplant tissues, organs, and glands. In order to perfect this approach, I started experimenting with tissue transplants on animals.

"I have observed for a long time the animals I operated on in my laboratory, trying to understand and learn what was happening to the organs moved to a new, sometimes unusual place. When my observations were over, the animal was transferred to the garden. That was how my garden-museum came about. I was particularly interested in the problem of exchange and transplantation of tissues between distant species – for example, between fish and mammals, and vise versa. In this area, I accomplished what scientists considered impossible. But what is so unusual about it? What I did today, tomorrow will be manageable by ordinary surgeons. Professor Shayne must be aware of the latest surgeries by the German Doctor Zauerbruch. He managed to replace a damaged hip with a calf."

"But what about Ichtiander?" the expert asked.

"Yes, Ichtiander is my crowning achievement. The difficulty in Ichtiander's operation was not only about the technique. I had to change the workings of the entire organism. Six monkeys died during the preliminary experiments, before I achieved my goal and was able to operate on the child without being worried about his safety."

"What was the nature of the operation?" the judge asked.

"I transplanted gills of a young child into the boy, and the child received the ability to live both on land and in the water."

Exclamations of surprise once again rippled through the audience. Reporters from various papers rushed to the phones to inform their publishers of this news.

"Later, I managed to achieve an even greater success. My latest project – the amphibian monkey you saw, can live indefinitely on land and underwater without any damage to itself. Ichtiander can only exist out of water three or four days. Prolonged presence on dry land is harmful to him – his lungs become fatigued and his gills dry up, at which point Ichtiander experiences stabbing pain in his sides. Unfortunately, during my absence, Ichtiander violated the regime I set up for him. He spent too much time on land, over worked his lungs, and has developed a serious illness. The balance in his body has been violated and now he must spend most of his time in the water. From the amphibian man he is slowly turning into a fish man."

"May I ask a question to the defendant?" the prosecutor said, addressing the judge. "How did Salvator come up with the idea of creating the amphibian man, and what was his purpose?"

"The idea was the same – man is not perfect. Having received great advantages compared to his animal ancestors in the course of evolution, we have, at the same time, lost much of what we had from lower stages of our animal development. Living in the water could give us tremendous advantages. Why can't we give this ability back to human beings? From the history of animal development we know that all land-bound animals and birds originated from the water – they emerged from the ocean. We know that some land animals returned to it. The dolphins started off as fish, came out on land, turned into a mammal, but then returned to the water and remained a mammal, like whales. The whales and the dolphins both have lungs. We could help the dolphins become an amphibian. Ichtiander asked me about it – then his friend, dolphin Leading, could stay underwater longer. I was planning to do this surgery on the dolphin. The first fish among men, and the first man among fish, Ichtiander couldn't help but feel lonely. But if other people followed him into the ocean, life would be completely different. Then people could easily defeat this mighty element – water. Do you know what sort of power it has? Are you aware that the area covered by the ocean equals almost one hundred and forty million square miles? Over seventy percent of Earth's surface is covered by the ocean. But this expanse with its vast stores of food and raw materials could accommodate millions, billions of people. A hundred and forty million square miles is just the surface. Billions of people could live in the ocean without feeling cramped or restricted.

"And its power! Did you know that ocean absorbs the amount of solar energy equivalent to nine billion horsepowers? Had it not been for the heat transfer to the air and other dissipations of heat, the ocean would have long since boiled. It is practically a limitless source of energy? How is it being used by the land-bound humanity? Virtually not at all.

"What about the power of waves and tides! The power of impact delivered by the waves can reach seventy-eight hundred pounds per square foot, the height of the surf can reach a hundred and forty feet, and the waves can lift up to three million pounds – rocks for instance. The tides can reach the height of over fifty feet – the height of a four-story building. How are we using these forces? We are not.

"On dry land, living creatures cannot rise very far above its surface or penetrate very deep under it. In the ocean, life is everywhere – from the equator to the poles, from the surface to the depth of nearly six and a half miles.

"How do we use the limitless wealth of the ocean? We fish. Or, I would say, we pick what's at the very surface of the ocean, leaving the depths completely unutilized. We gather sponges, corals, pearls and seaweed – and nothing more.

"We do some work underwater – build supports for bridges and dams, raise sunken ships, and that's all! We do all this with great difficulty, with great risk, sometimes with human casualties. A poor land-bound human dies underwater after two minutes! You can't do much work with that.

"How different it would be, if a person could live and work underwater without a scuba suit and oxygen tanks.

"How many treasures he could discover! Take Ichtiander, for instance… But I am afraid to tease the demon of human greed. Ichtiander often brought me samples of rare metals and minerals from the ocean floor. Oh, don't worry, he only brought me small samples, but their deposits in the ocean could be tremendous.

"And what of the sunken treasure?

"Remember the ocean liner *Lusitania*. In the spring of nineteen sixteen it was sunk by the Germans near the shores of Ireland. In addition to the valuables belonging to the fifteen hundred perished passengers, *Lusitania* carried a hundred and fifty million dollars in gold coin and fifty million dollars' worth of gold. (There were gasps in the audience.) In addition, there were two boxes of diamonds destined for Amsterdam. Among the diamonds was one of the best in the world – diamond *Caliph* worth many millions. Of course, even someone like Ichtiander could not descend to great depths – we would have to create a man (There was a cry of indignation from the prosecutor) to be able to sustain great pressure, like the deep-sea fish. Although, I don't see anything impossible about that. But, all in good time."

"You appear to see yourself as an all-mighty deity, don't you?" the prosecutor noted.

Salvator pay no attention to this remark and continued, "If people could live in water, then exploration of the ocean and its depth would have moved in giant strides. The sea would no longer be a menacing force demanding human sacrifice. We would no longer have to mourn the drowned."

Everyone in the audience seemed to already envision the underwater world, conquered by mankind. What benefits it promised! Even the judge couldn't help himself and asked, "Then why didn't you publish the results of your experiments?"

"I was in no hurry to end up in court," Salvator replied with a smile, "and, besides, I was afraid that my inventions would bring more harm than good in the existing society. Struggle has already ensued around Ichtiander. Who reported me out of spite? Zurita, who kidnapped Ichtiander from me. Even worse, Ichtiander could have been taken from Zurita by admirals and generals, to force the amphibian man to sink military ships. No, I could not make Ichtiander and his like communal property in a country where struggle and greed turn the greatest discoveries into evil, increasing the sum of human suffering. I have thought of..."

Salvator paused then changed his tone abruptly and continued, "I will not talk about that. Otherwise I will be declared mad." Salvator smiled at the expert. "No, I decline the honor of being a madman, albeit a genius one. I am not a madman or a maniac. Didn't I make my ideas reality? You have seen all my work with your own eyes. If you believe my actions to be criminal, then try me in accordance to the law. I ask for no indulgence."

IN PRISON

The experts who examined Ichtiander were tasked with not only paying attention to his physical condition, but also to his mental capacity.

"What year is it? What month? What date? Day of the week?" the experts asked.

Ichtiander replied, "I don't know."

He had difficulty answering the simplest questions. But he could not be declared retarded. There were many things he didn't know due to the peculiar circumstances of his existence and upbringing. He was like a big child. The experts concluded that Ichtiander was mentally incompetent. This freed him from legal responsibility. The court dropped the case against Ichtiander and sought to establish guardianship. Two people expressed desire to be Ichtiander's guardians – Zurita and Balthazar.

Salvator was right when he stated that Zurita reported him out of spite. But Zurita was not just getting back at Salvator for losing Ichtiander. Zurita was pursuing another goal – he wanted to have sole charge of

Ichtiander by becoming his guardian. Zurita spared a dozen valuable pearls and bribed the members of the court and guardianship council. He was now close to his goal.

Citing his fatherhood, Balthazar demanded to have guardianship rights bestowed upon him. But he was out of luck. Despite all of Larra's efforts, the experts stated they could not establish the link between Ichtiander and Balthazar's son born twenty years prior, based on the testimony of one witness – Christo. Besides, he was Balthazar's brother and inspired no trust in the experts.

Larra did not know that the prosecutor and the bishop also became involved in the case. They needed Balthazar in court as a victim, as a father, whose son was kidnapped and disfigured. But to acknowledge Balthazar's parenthood legally and give him Ichtiander was not in the court's and church's plans – they wanted to be rid of Ichtiander altogether.

Christo moved in with his brother and was becoming worried about him. Balthazar remained deep in thought for hours on end, forgetting about sleep and food. Then, sometimes, he became extremely agitated, dashed around the shop and shouted, "My son! My son!" At such moments he cursed the Spaniards with every oath in every language he knew."

Once, after one such fit, Balthazar suddenly declared to Christo, "Listen, brother, I am going to prison. I shall give my best pearls to the guards to allow me to see Ichtiander. I shall speak to him. He must recognize me as his father. A son cannot forget his father. My blood must tell him so."

As much as Christo tried to talk his brother out of it, nothing helped. Balthazar was unmoved.

He went to prison.

He begged the guards, cried, groveled before them, pleaded with them and, finally, having scattered the path from the gates to the prison entrance with pearls, he made it to Ichtiander's cell.

This small space, barely lit with a narrow grated window, was stuffy and ill-smelling; the prison guards changed the water in the cistern infrequently and took no trouble to remove rotting fish from the floor – the only food offered to the unusual prisoner.

A metal cistern stood by the wall across from the window.

Balthazar walked up to the cistern and looked at the dark surface of water hiding Ichtiander.

"Ichtiander!" Balthazar called out. "Ichtiander," he repeated.

The water surface rippled, but the boy did not appear.

Having waited a little longer, Balthazar reached out with a shaking hand and lowered it into the warm water. His fingers found a shoulder.

Ichtiander's wet head suddenly appeared from the cistern. He rose up to his shoulders and asked, "Who is it? What do you want?"

Balthazar fell to his knees and spoke quickly, reaching out his hands, "Ichtiander! Your father is here. Your real father. Salvator is not your father. He is a wicked man. He disfigured you. Ichtiander! Ichtiander! Look at me closely. Don't you recognize your father?"

Water ran slowly down the boy's thick hair onto his pale face and ripped from his chin. He gazed at the old Indian sadly and with some surprise.

"I don't know you," he said.

"Ichtiander," Balthazar shouted, "look at me closely!" And the old Indian suddenly grabbed the young man's head, drew him closer and started covering his face with kisses, tears spilling from his eyes.

Fighting away this unexpected gesture, Ichtiander splashed in the cistern, spilling water over the edge onto the stone floor.

Someone's hand grabbed the back of Balthazar's neck, lifted him and threw him into the corner. Balthazar crashed to the floor, painfully hitting his head against the stone wall.

When he opened his eyes, Balthazar saw Zurita standing over him. His right fist clenched, Zurita was holding a piece of paper in his left, shaking it triumphantly.

"See? This is the order appointing me Ichtiander's guardian. You will have to find a wealthy son elsewhere. I am taking this young man with me tomorrow morning. Understand?"

Balthazar, still sprawled on the floor, growled dully and menacingly.

The next moment, Balthazar jumped to his feet and attacked his enemy with a savage scream, knocking him off his feet.

The Indian snatched the piece of paper from Zurita, stuffed it into his mouth and continued beating up the Spaniard. A cruel fight ensued.

The prison guard standing by the door with the keys in his hands, considered it necessary to observe strict neutrality. He received large bribes from both men and didn't want to interfere. Only when Zurita started strangling the old man, the guard became worried, "Hey, don't kill him!"

The enraged Zurita paid no attention to the guard's warning, and Balthazar would have been in trouble, had another person not appeared in the cell.

"Splendid! The guardian is practicing his guardianship rights!" Salvator's voice sounded. "What are you looking at? Don't you know your duties?" Salvator shouted at the guard as if he was the warden.

Salvator's command had its effect. The guard ran in to separate the fighters.

Other guards rushed in, and soon Zurita and Balthazar were dragged in opposite directions.

Zurita could consider himself the victor. But the defeated Salvator was still stronger than his opponents. Even there, in the cell, in the position of a prisoner, Salvator never seized controlling people and events.

"Take these troublemakers out of the cell," Salvator ordered, addressing the guards. "I must be alone with Ichtiander." The guards obeyed. Despite protests and cursing, Zurita and Balthazar were taken away. The cell door slammed shut.

As soon as the voices faded down the corridor, Salvator approached the cistern and said to Ichtiander peeking from the water, "Stand up, Ichtiander. Step out into the middle of the cell, I need to examine you."

The young man obeyed.

"Good," Salvator continued, "closer to the light. Breathe. Deeper. More. Hold your breath. Right."

Salvator tapped on Ichtiander's chest and listened to the boy's halting breathing.

"Are you short of breath?"

"Yes, father," Ichtiander replied.

"It's your own fault," Salvator said. "You shouldn't have stayed on land so much."

Ichtiander lowered his head and thought. He then looked up and looking into Salvator's eyes said, "Father, but why can't I? Why everyone can, but I can't?"

Salvator was hard pressed tolerating this gaze filled with hidden reproach. It was much more difficult than testifying at the trial. But Salvator withstood it.

"Because you have what no other person has – the ability to live underwater. If you were given a choice, Ichtiander, to be like everyone else and live on land or to live solely underwater, what would you choose?"

"I don't know..." the boy replied after a pause. The underwater world and land with Gutierre on it were equally precious to him. But Gutierre was lost to him.

"Now, I would prefer the ocean," the boy replied.

"You have already made this choice, Ichtiander, when you disrupted your inner balance through your disobedience. Now you can only live underwater."

"But not in this terrible dirty water, father. I will die here. I want to be in the ocean!"

Salvator suppressed a sigh.

"I will do everything I can to free you from this prison, Ichtiander. Be brave!" He patted the boy's shoulder, left Ichtiander and returned to his cell.

Having settled down onto a stool by the narrow table, Salvator fell deep into thought.

Like any surgeon, he had known failure. Many lives were lost under his scalpel from his own errors, before he reached perfection. However, he never thought about those victims. Dozens died, but thousands were saved. He was quite satisfied with this arithmetic.

However, he considered himself responsible for Ichtiander's fate. Ichtiander was his pride. He loved the boy as his best work. Besides, he became attached to Ichtiander and came to love him as a son. Presently, Salvator was preoccupied with Ichtiander's illness and his further destiny.

Someone knocked on the cell door.

"Come in!" Salvator said.

"Have I disturbed you, Professor?" the prison warden asked quietly.

"Not at all," Salvator replied, rising. "How are your wife and baby?"

"They are well, thank you. I sent him to my mother-in-law, far away from here, to the Andes."

"Yes, mountain climate will do them some good," Salvator replied. The warden didn't leave. Glancing at the door, he walked up to Salvator and said quietly, "Professor, I owe you my life for saving my wife. I love her as..."

"Don't thank me, it was my job."

"I cannot be indebted to you," the warden replied. "And there is more. I am an ignorant man. But I read papers and know what Professor Salvator means. I cannot allow for a man like that to be held in prison with vagrants and highway robbers."

"My scientific friends," Salvator said with a smile, "may have succeeded at getting me into a clinic as a mental patient."

"A prison clinic is no better than prison," the warden objected. "It's even worse. Instead of brigands you'll be surrounded by madmen. Salvator among the insane! No, this must not be!"

Once again lowering his voice to a whisper, the warden continued, "I have thought it all through. There is a reason I sent my family to the mountains. I can now arrange an escape for you and disappear myself. I was forced here by poverty, but I hate this job. They'll never find me and you... you can leave this accursed country ran by priests and merchants. There is something else I want to tell you," he continued after some hesitation. "I am giving away a state secret..."

"Perhaps you shouldn't," Salvator interrupted.

"Yes, but... I can't... First of all I myself cannot carry out the terrible order they gave me. My conscience would torture me for the rest of my life. You have done so much for me, and they... I owe nothing to the authorities pushing me to commit a crime."

"Indeed?" Salvator asked.

"Yes, I found out that Ichtiander won't be given either to Balthazar or to the guardian, Zurita, even though Zurita already has an authorization. Even Zurita won't get him, despite his generous bribes because... it's been decided to kill Ichtiander."

Salvator made a slight gesture.

"Indeed? Continue!"

"Yes, kill Ichtiander – the bishop insisted the most, even though he never said the word 'kill.' I was given some poison, I think it's potassium cyanide. Tonight, I must add the poison to the water in Ichtiander's cistern. The prison doctor has been bribed. He will testify that Ichtiander died from the surgery you conducted to turn him into the amphibian man.

148

If I don't carry out the order, I will be dealt with ruthlessly. And I have a family. They'll kill me too, and no one will know. I am completely at their mercy. I have a crime in my past, a small, almost accidental one. I was going to flee anyway and had everything ready. But I can't, I don't want to kill Ichtiander. Saving both of you in such a short time is difficult, almost impossible. But I can save you. I have thought about it. I feel sorry for Ichtiander, but your life is more important. You can use your art to create another Ichtiander, but no one in the world can create another Salvator."

Salvator walked up to the warden, shook his hand and said, "I thank you, but I cannot accept this sacrifice for myself. You might be caught and put on trial."

"There is no sacrifice! I have thought about everything."

"Wait. I said I cannot accept it for myself. But if you save Ichtiander, you will do more for me than if you get me out. I am healthy, strong, and have friends everywhere who can help set me free. But Ichtiander must be saved immediately."

"I accept this as your order," the warden said. When he left, Salvator smiled and said, "That's better. May no one get the golden apple." Salvator paced around the room, quietly whispered, "Poor boy!" walked up to the desk, wrote something down, then knocked on his door.

"Please ask the warden to come back."

When the warden returned, Salvator said, "I have one more request. Could you arrange for me to meet with Ichtiander – one last time?"

"Easily! None of my superiors are here, and the entire prison is at our disposal."

"Excellent. And one more thing."

"I am at your service."

"By freeing Ichtiander, you will be doing a lot for me."

"But you have done me such service, Professor..."

"Let's assume we are even," Salvator interrupted. "But I can and want to help your family. Here is a note. It only has an address and one letter 'S' for Salvator. Go to this address. I trust this man. If you need to hide somewhere temporarily or help with money..."

"But..."

"No buts. Please, take me to Ichtiander."

Ichtiander was surprised to see Salvator in his cell. He had never seen him as sad and gentle as this time.

"Ichtiander, son," Salvator said. "We are going to have to part ways sooner than I thought and possibly for a long time. Your fate troubles me. You are surrounded by a thousand perils. If you remain here, you might die, or, at best, end up in the hands of Zurita or another predator like him."

"What about you, father?"

"The court will find me guilty, of course, and put me away into prison, where I will probably spend a couple of years, possibly more. While I am in prison, you must be someplace safe and as far from here as possible. There is a place like that, but it is very far from here, on the other side of South America, to the west, in the Pacific Ocean, on one of the Tuamotu Islands. It won't be easy getting there, but the dangers of your voyage are still less than those that threaten you here, at home, or at the La Plata Bay. It's easier to go and find the islands than avoid the nets and traps of your cunning enemies.

"Which route should you take? You can go there by a northern or a southern route. Both have their advantages and drawbacks. The northern route is somewhat longer. In addition, by choosing it, you would have to go from the Atlantic to the Pacific Ocean through the Panama Canal, which is dangerous – you could be caught, especially at the locks or, at the slightest mistake, you could be crushed by a ship. The canal is not very wide or deep – just under three hundred feet at its widest point, and forty-one feet at the deepest. The latest ocean liners almost touch its bottom with their keels.

"However, by the northern route you will always remain in warm waters. Besides, there are three large oceanic routes going to the west from the Panama Canal – two leading toward New Zealand and one toward Fiji and beyond. By choosing the middle one and watching the ships, or possibly holding on to them, you could get almost all the way to your destination. Both routes to New Zealand are in the vicinity of the Tuamotu Islands. You would only have to travel north a little bit.

"The southern route is shorter, but you will be traveling in the cold southern currents, by the floating ice boundary, especially when you go around Cape Horn at Terra del Fuego – the southernmost point of South America. The Magellan Straight is very stormy.

"Of course, it's not as dangerous for you as it is for sail ships and steam boats, but it is dangerous nonetheless. It used to be a real cemetery of sail ships. It is wide at the eastern end and narrow at the western end, as well as scattered with rocks and small islands. Strong western winds propel the water to the east – in the opposite direction from the one you'll be taking. You could crash in the underwater whirlpool. Which is why I would advise to lengthen the trip and go around Cape Horn instead of through the Magellan Straight. Water turns cold gradually and I hope you'll get used to it and remain healthy. You won't have to worry about food – it's always on hand as well as water. You have been drinking sea water since childhood without any damage to your health.

"It will be somewhat more difficult to find the way from Cape Horn to the Tuamotu Islands, compared to traveling from the Panama Canal. There are no large oceanic routes from Cape Horn to the north, not a lot of traffic. I shall give you the exact longitude and latitude – you will check them using the special tools made for you following my instructions. But these tools will slow you down some and constrict your movements."

"I shall take Leading. He will carry the tools. How could I leave him behind? He has probably been missing me."

"I don't know who has been missing whom more," Salvator smiled again. "Well then, Leading it is. Excellent. You'll make it to the Tuamotu Islands. Then you'll have to find a secluded coral atoll. Its landmark is a tall mast, with a weather vane in the shape of a large fish at the top. It's easy to remember. Perhaps you'll spend a month looking for this island, or two, or three – it's not a problem. Water there is warm, and there are plenty of oysters."

Salvator had disciplined Ichtiander to listen patiently, without interrupting, but when Salvator reached this point in his explanation, Ichtiander couldn't help himself, "What will I find on the island with the fish weather vane?"

"Friends. Good friends, their care and kindness," Salvator replied. "An old friend of mine lives there – scientist Armand Vilbois, a Frenchman and a famous oceanographer. I met him and became friends with him when I was in Europe many years ago. Armand Vilbois is the most interesting man, but I don't have time to tell you about him right now. I hope you'll come to know him for yourself and discover what brought him to a lonely coral atoll in the Pacific Ocean. He is not alone. He has a wife, a sweet, kind woman, a son and a daughter. The latter was born on the island, and is now seventeen. His son is twenty-five.

"They know about you from my letters and I am certain they will accept you into their family like one of their own..." Salvator paused. "Of course, now you will have to spend most of your time in the water. But you can come out to the shore for several hours every day, enough for friendly meetings and conversations. It's possible that your health will improve, and you'll be able to stay on land as long as in the water.

"Armand Vilbois will be like a second father to you. And you'll be an irreplaceable aide in his scientific work in oceanography. What you know about the ocean and its dwellers is enough for ten professors." Salvator chuckled. "The silly experts followed a standard method by asking you at the trial, what was the day, or the month, or the date, and you couldn't answer because it was of no interest to you. Had they at least asked you about underwater currents, water temperature, and salt content in the La Plata Bay and its vicinity – your answers could have made up an entire volume. There is so much more you'll be able to learn – and later communicate your knowledge to others – when your underwater excursions are guided by an experienced and brilliant scientist like Armand Vilbois. The two of you, I am certain, will create a book on oceanography that would equal an entire era in the development of this science, and will become world-famous. Your name will be next to that of Armand Vilbois – I know him, he will insist upon it. You will serve science and, thus all of mankind.

"But if you stay here, you will be forced to serve the basest interests of ignorant, greedy people. I am confident that in the clear, transparent waters of the atoll and in the family of Armand Vilbois you will find your quiet haven and be happy.

"One more advice.

"As soon as you are out in the ocean – and this might take place as soon as tonight – swim home immediately through the underwater tunnel. The only person there right now is my faithful Jim. Take the navigation instruments, the knife and other things, find Leading, and be on your way before sunrise.

"Farewell, Ichtiander! No, until we meet again!"

For the first time in his life, Salvator hugged and kissed Ichtiander. Then he smiled, clapped the boy on the shoulder and said, "A man like you will get through anything!" and quickly left the cell.

THE ESCAPE

Olsen had only just returned from the button factory and sat down to dinner. Someone knocked.

"Who is it?" Olsen shouted, unhappy about the interruption. The door opened and Gutierre came in.

"Gutierre! You? Where are you coming from?" Olsen exclaimed, surprised and happy, as he rose from the chair.

"Hello, Olsen" Gutierre said. "Continue your dinner." Leaning against the door, Gutierre announced, "I can't live with my husband and his mother anymore. Zurita... he dared to hit me. And I left him. I left him for good, Olsen." This news made Olsen interrupt his dinner once again.

"What a surprise!" he exclaimed. "Sit! You are barely standing. But how is it possible? You always said, 'What God united no man can pull apart'. And you left him? All the better. I am glad. Did you go back to your father?"

"My father doesn't know. Zurita would have found me there and forced me back. I am staying with a friend."

"And... and what are you going to do next?"

"I will work at the factory. I came to ask you, Olsen, to help me find work at the factory, I don't care what kind." Olsen shook his head anxiously, "It's very difficult right now. Of course, I'll try."

Olsen paused and asked, "What will your husband think about it?"

"I don't care."

"But he will care to know where his wife is at," Olsen said with a smile. "Don't forget, you are in Argentina. Zurita will find you and then... You know he won't leave you alone. The law and public opinion are on his side."

Gutierre thought about it and said firmly, "Very well! Then I'll go to Canada, to Alaska..."

"To Greenland, to the North Pole!" Then Olsen said more seriously, "We'll think about it. It's not safe for you to stay here. I have long since been trying to get out of here myself. Why did I come here, to Latin America? The church spirit is still too strong here. It's a pity we couldn't get away the last time. But Zurita managed to kidnap you, and our tickets and money were lost. Now you probably don't have the money to sail to Europe, and neither do I. But we don't have to go to Europe right away. If we – and I say 'we' because I won't leave you until you are

153

someplace safe – if we make it at least to Paraguay or, better yet, to Brazil, Zurita will have a harder time finding you, and we'll have time to prepare for a trip to the States or to Europe. Did you know Doctor Salvator was in prison, along with Ichtiander?"

"Ichtiander? They found him? Why is he in prison? Can I see him?" Gutierre showered Olsen with questions.

"Yes, Ichtiander is in prison, and he might once again end up being Zurita's slave. It's a ridiculous trial with ridiculous accusations against Salvator and Ichtiander."

"That is terrible! Is it impossible to save him?"

"I kept trying but without success. Unexpectedly, the prison warden himself turned out to be our ally. Tonight, we are going to free Ichtiander. I have just received two short notes – one from Salvator and another one from the warden."

"I want to see Ichtiander!" Gutierre said. "Can I come with you?"

Olsen thought.

"I don't think so," he replied. "And it's better if you didn't see Ichtiander."

"But why?"

"Because Ichtiander is sick. He is sick as a man, although healthy as a fish."

"I don't understand."

"Ichtiander can't be on dry land anymore. What will happen when he sees you again? It will be very difficult for him and, perhaps, for you. Ichtiander will want to stay with you, and life on land will kill him."

Gutierre hung her head.

"Yes, I think you might be right," she said after a pause.

"The insurmountable barrier – the ocean – now lies between him and other people. Ichtiander is doomed. From now on, water has to be his one and only home."

"But how will he live there? Alone in the limitless ocean – a man among the fish and sea monsters?"

"He was happy in his underwater world before..." Gutierre blushed.

"Now of course, he won't be quite as happy as before."

"Stop it, Olsen," Gutierre said sadly.

"Time heals all wounds. Perhaps he will recover his lost peace. And live among the fish and sea monsters. If a shark doesn't get him before his time, he might live to a good old age. And death? Death is the same everywhere."

Twilight was falling and the room was almost dark.

"It's time," Olsen said, rising. Gutierre rose too.

"Can I see him at least from a distance?" Gutierre asked.

"Of course, as long as you don't betray your presence."

"Yes, I promise."

It was completely dark when Olsen, dressed as a cab driver, guided his cart into the prison yard from Coronel Dias. The guard at the gates called out to him, "Where are you going?"

"I am bringing water for the Sea Devil," Olsen replied, as he was told by the prison warden.

All guards knew that there was an unusual prisoner held in one of the cell – the Sea Devil who lived in the cistern filled with sea water because he couldn't stand fresh water. The water was changed from time to time. It was brought in a large barrel set on a horse-drawn cart.

Olsen drove up to the prison building, turned around the corner where the kitchen was located, as well as the entrance for the prison staff. The warden had everything ready. The guards usually watching the corridor and the entrance were sent away on various errands. Ichtiander accompanied by the warden walked out unchallenged.

"Come on, jump into the tank, quickly!" the warden said. Ichtiander wasted no time.

"Go!"

Olsen flipped the reins, left the prison yard and slowly followed Aveni da Alvar, past Ritero railway station.

Following him, a woman's shadow flickered a short distance away.

It was the middle of the night when Olsen left the city. The road followed the sea coast. Wind was getting stronger. Waves rushed onto the shore and crashed noisily over the rocks.

Olsen glanced around. There was no one on the road. In the distance, he saw the approaching headlights of a swiftly moving car. "Let it drive by."

Roaring and blinding him with the lights, the car zoomed by toward the city and vanished in the distance.

"It's time!" Olsen turned and gestured to Gutierre to hide behind the rocks. He then knocked on the barrel and shouted, "We are here! Climb out!"

A head appeared from the barrel.

Ichtiander looked around, quickly climbed out and humped onto the ground.

"Thank you, Olsen!" the young man said, firmly shaking the giant's hand with his own wet hand.

Ichtiander was breathing haltingly, as if during an asthma attack.

"Not at all. Farewell! Be careful. Don't get too close to the shore. Stay away from people, or else you might get caught again."

Even Olsen didn't know about the instructions Ichtiander received from Salvator.

"Yes, yes," Ichtiander said gasping. "I shall go far-far away, to quiet coral atolls, where not a single ship comes to visit. Thank you, Olsen!" and the boy ran to the sea.

By the water's edge, he suddenly turned and shouted, "Olsen, Olsen! If you ever see Gutierre, give her my love and tell her that I shall never forget her!" He dove into the sea, shouted, "Farewell, Gutierre!" and disappeared underwater.

"Farewell, Ichtiander..." Gutierre said quietly, standing behind the rocks.

The wind grew even stronger, almost knocking them off their feet. The sea raged, the sand hissed, the rocks thundered.

Someone's hand clasped Gutierre's.

"Come, Gutierre!" Olsen said gently. He led Gutierre to the road.

Gutierre glanced back at the sea one more time and headed toward the city, leaning on Olsen's arm.

***

Salvator served his sentence and resumed his scientific studies. He is now preparing for a long trip.

Christo continues to serve him.

Zurita bought a new schooner and is now looking for pearls in the California Bay. While he is not the wealthiest man in America, he cannot complain. The tips of his mustache, like barometer hands, show high pressure.

Gutierre divorced her husband and married Olsen. They moved to New York and both work at a canning factory. At the La Plata coast no one remembers the Sea Devil any longer.

Only sometimes, during hot nights, the old fishermen hear a strange sound in the silence and say to the young ones, "The Sea Devil used to play his trumpet like that," and start telling legends about him.

Only one man in Buenos Aires cannot forget Ichtiander. All street urchins in town know the old, poor, half-mad Indian.

"There goes the Sea Devil's father!"

But the Indian pays them no attention.

Whenever he meets a Spaniard, the old man turns, spits after him and mumbles a curse.

But the police don't bother old Balthazar. His madness is of the quiet kind, and he doesn't harm anyone.

When the seas turn stormy, the old Indian becomes extremely agitated.

He rushes to the shore and at the risk of being swept off by the waves, stands on the rocks, and shouts, shouts day and night, until the storm subsides, "Ichtiander! Ichtiander! My son!"

But the sea keeps its secret safe.

ABOUT THE AUTHOR

Alexander Romanovich Belyaev was born in 1884 in Smolensk, in the family of a Russian Orthodox minister. His sister Nina and brother Vasily both died young and tragically.

Following the wishes of his father, Alexander graduated the local seminary but decided not to become a minister. On the contrary, he graduated a passionate atheist. After the seminary he entered a law school in Yaroslavl. When his father died unexpectedly, Alexander had to find ways to make ends meet including tutoring, creating theater sets and playing violin in a circus orchestra.

Fortunately, his law studies did not go to waste. As soon as Belyaev graduated the law school, he established a private practice in his home town of Smolensk and soon acquired a reputation of a talented and shrewd attorney. He took advantage of the better income to travel, acquire a very respectable art collection and create a large library. Belyaev felt so secure, financially, that he got married and left his law practice to write full-time.

At the age of thirty-five Belyaev was faced with the most serious trial of his life. He became ill with Plevritis which, after an unsuccessful treatment attempt, developed into spinal tuberculosis and leg paralysis. His wife left him, unwilling to be tied to a sick man. Belyaev spent six years in bed, three of which – in a full-torso cast. Fortunately, the other two women in his life – his mother and his old nanny – refused to give up on him. They helped seek out specialists who could help him and took him away from the dismal climate of central Russia to Yalta – a famous Black Sea resort.

While at the hospital in Yalta, Belyaev started writing poetry. He also determined that, while he could not do much with his body, he had to do something with his mind. He read all he could find by Jules Verne, H.G. Wells and by the famous Russian scientist Tsiolkovsky. He studied languages, medicine, biology, history, and technical sciences.

No one had a clear idea how, but in 1922 Belyaev finally overcame his illness and returned to normal life and work. To cut the cost of living, Belyaev moved his family from the expensive Yalta to Moscow and took up law once again. At the same time, he put all the things he learned during the long years of his illness to use, by weaving them into fascinating adventure and science fiction plots. His works appeared more and more frequently in scientific magazines, quickly earning him the title of "Soviet Jules Verne".

After successfully publishing several full-length novels, he moved his family to St. Petersburg (then Leningrad) and once again became a full-time writer. Sadly, the cold damp climate had caused a relapse in Belyaev's health. Unwilling to jeopardize his family's finances by moving to yet another resort town, he compromised by moving them somewhat further south, where the cost of living was still reasonable – to Kiev.

The family didn't get to enjoy the better climes for long. In 1930 the writer's six-year old daughter died of meningitis, his second daughter contracted rickets, and his own illness once again grew worse.

The following years were full of ups and downs. There was the meeting with one of Belyaev's heroes – H.G. Wells in 1934. There was the parting of ways with the magazine Around the World after eleven years of collaboration. There was the controversial article *Cinderella* about the dismal state of science fiction at the time.

Shortly before the Great Patriotic War (June 22, 1941 – May 9, 1945), Alexander Romanovich went through yet another surgery and could not evacuate when the war began. The town of Pushkin, a St. Petersburg suburb, where Belyaev and his family lived, became occupied by the German troops. Belyaev died of hunger in January, 1942. A German general and four soldiers took his body away and buried it somewhere. It was highly irregular for the members of the German military to bury a dead Soviet citizen. When asked about it, the general explained that he used to enjoy Belyaev's books as a boy, and considered it his duty to bury him properly.

The exact place of Belyaev's burial is unknown to this day. After the war, the Kazan cemetery of the town of Pushkin received a commemorative stele as the sign of remembrance and respect for the great author.

ABOUT THE TRANSLATOR

Maria K. is the pen name of Maria Igorevna Kuroshchepova – a writer, translator, and blogger of Russian-Ukrainian decent. Maria came to the United States in 1994 as an impressionable 19-year old exchange student. She received her Bachelors and Masters degrees in engineering from Rochester Institute of Technology (Rochester, NY).

Maria covers a wide range of topics from travel and fashion to politics and social issues. Her science fiction and fantasy works include *Limited Time for Tomato Soup*, *The SHIELD*, *The Elemental Tales* and others.

A non-fiction and science fiction writer in her own right, Maria is also a prolific translator of less-known works of Russian and Soviet literature into English. Her most prominent translations include her grandfather Vasily Kuznetsov's Siege of Leningrad journals titled *The Ring of Nine*, and *Thais of Athens* – a historic novel by Ivan Yefremov. Both works quickly made their way into the top 100 Kindle publications in their respective categories and continue attracting consistent interest and acclaim from readers.